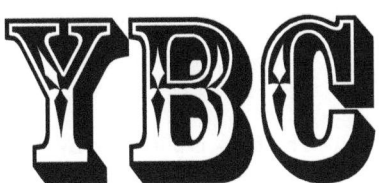

Leon J. Gratton

Grosvenor House
Publishing Limited

All rights reserved
Copyright © Leon J. Gratton, 2025

The right of Leon J. Gratton to be identified as the author of this
work has been asserted in accordance with Section 78
of the Copyright, Designs and Patents Act 1988

The book cover is copyright to Leon J. Gratton

This book is published by
Grosvenor House Publishing Ltd
Link House
140 The Broadway, Tolworth, Surrey, KT6 7HT.
www.grosvenorhousepublishing.co.uk

This book is sold subject to the conditions that it shall not, by way of
trade or otherwise, be lent, resold, hired out or otherwise circulated
without the author's or publisher's prior consent in any form of
binding or cover other than that in which it is published and
without a similar condition including this condition being
imposed on the subsequent purchaser.

This book is a work of fiction. Any resemblance to
people or events, past or present, is purely coincidental.

A CIP record for this book
is available from the British Library

ISBN 978-1-83615-152-4

To my son Darren

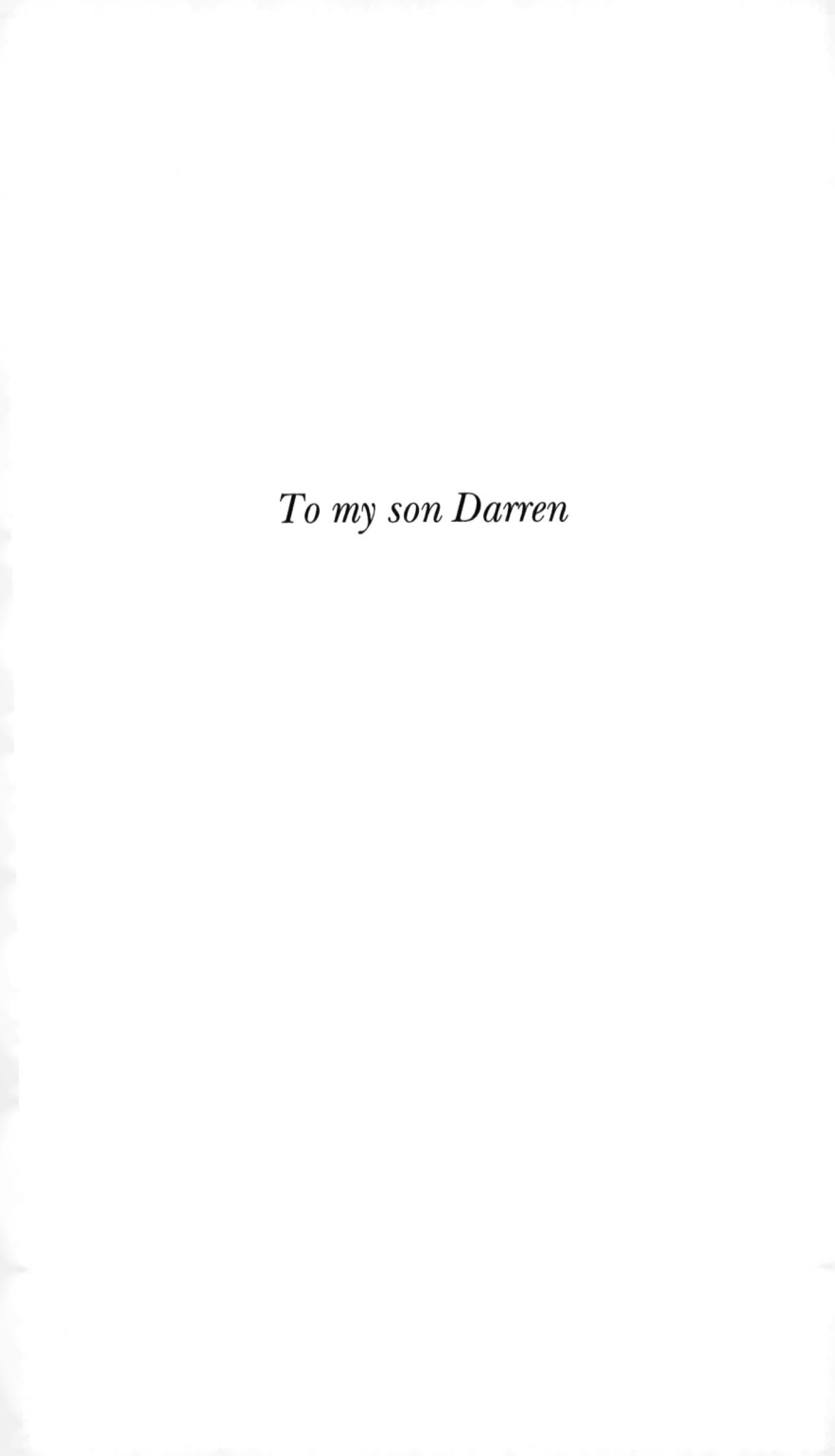

CHAPTER

Grandad woke that morning with a dry mouth and went straight away and got himself a drink of water. He smiled, he could hear his mam gently snoring in the room through the wall. He smiled, as the woman was a saint and if she found out half the shit, he had been up to then she would have clasped the cuffs on him herself. But secrets he was an expert at hiding things. Anyway, he smiled as he produced a Regal fag and lit it up inhaling the smoke into his lungs and getting his morning rush. He took out his stash and smiled knowing that it was tick day. Most of the people he dealt with were lay-on's. He didn't mind as they were pretty good at coughing up, He smiled and counted out his readies, these totalled about eight hundred pounds. He was due just under a grand and the eight hundred was just enough for him to invest in more product. He would meet his main man later and he had a pretty positive feeling about the score. He knew he was getting a shit load of Eckies, these were Hearts and Mitsubishis. The hearts weighed in at fifteen pound a pill and were pure beautiful.

He walked down to his muckers house in Sighthill, everything was quiet since the war with the Skulls. Grandad was, as were the rest of the Y.B.C., proud of their win in the street war. But this didn't mean they could slack off, especially in the Cocaine world. No, they had to run a tight ship and the Bobbies were constantly watching and waiting for them to slip up. He sighed and rapped on the door of Pinkie.

Giz's voice sailed through the house, "its Grandad," he shouted then opened the door.

Gramps smiled and held out his hand. "How much am I due yae?"

Grandad smiled and replied, "Sixty for the Eckies and sixty for the two gramme of white".

Giz smiled then went into his room for the monies. He came back and handed the money over. Grandad smiled through his teeth and said, "You want a couple of Hearts?"

Giz smiled and replied, "How much?"

Grandad nodded his head "Fifteen a pop."

Giz smiled and replied, "okay gies two".

Grandad fished in his pocket and handed over two heart shaped pills. "Ideal for snorting," he said.

Gizmo smiled at this.

Pinkie slipped on his jumper and came to see Grandad.

"Awright Pinkie?" Came the question from Grandad.

"Aye I'm No bad."

Grandad sniffed in with attitude. "Am I due you anything?" asked Pinkie.

Grandad rolled his eyeballs up into his eye sockets, "Aye fifty quid," he said and Pinkie smiled.

"I don't know how you carry on with all that tick in your head, but as usual you are bang on," he handed Grandad two twenties and a ten.

Grandad pocketed the money and lit up a fag. "You two up tae anything?"

Pinkie smiled and snorted a half laugh "Na man." he said then continued. "We were thinking about going to the meadows there is a hippy fest on today".

Grandad nodded, "lots of drugs and lots of babes".

Pinkie smiled, "Well it's a sunny day and the drugs at the thing are phenomenal."

Grandad laughed, "Theres nae need to sell it tae me, I was sold at the drugs part".

Gizmo smiled. "We'll need dope and beer," he said then went and got dressed.

"Whose holding?". Grandad smiled and said, "That'll be Biscuit".

Giz smiled again and went. "I've got a crack bubble, you got any coke?"

Grandad nodded his head. "Yeah man I got some nice Bolivian gold flake".

Giz gripped his wrist and he said, "My man".

Gramps had never been a day without a turnover of product, not since the end of the sugar wars. They had made their mark and enforced it with much resolve. Pinkie was set free as were Nichol and Becksy. They were greeted by the streets with much enthusiasm. Coming home with a conqueror's reputation. The three of them were received and didn't have to shell out a single penny.

Grandad smiled as the pub 'The Gauntlet' got a new owner. Grandad was counting the days as to when they would strike at the pub again. Kingo was silent yet smiling at the thought of another free bar. But this owner was tough and I mean tough. It was reputed that the owner had a shotgun behind the counter. Grandad laughed at this as it only made it more a challenge for the Y.B.C. Kingo as usual had plans within plans. He was sly as a fox but dangerous as a wolf. It was only a matter of time before he went head-to-head with the new owner. Nessy was rubbing his hands in glee at the prospect of another free bar. Grandad Pinkie and Giz. Got on a bus to the centre of Edinburgh. They had stopped at Biscuits door for a lump of Tarrie. It was a half-ounce and they knew that it would last the three of them and that was why they were in high spirits.

Grandad skinned up soon as the bus departed the stop and headed towards Lothian Road. Grandad produced the giant Rizla and skinned a three skinner that was a miniature baseball bat. He packed it with dope and lit the thing and the whole bus was high, as the tarrie wafted through out the top deck of the bus. Grandad inhaled the joint then handed it to Gizmo. Gizmo drew in a nice inhalation of the dope it was black, red seal. And was pungent yet sweet at the same time. They got closer to their destination and the dope was nice. The weather well it was sweet, and anything could happen on a day like this. Grandad smiled as the joint came close to the roach and they were pretty much wasted. Grandad rang the bell and they got off just adjacent the meadows.

They headed into the Lothian Roadside and cut across the Meadows. Grandad smiled as he could hear the cheer as a band that sounded like Echo and the Bunnymen played their set. Grandad sat down amongst the stoned and the getting stoned. He smiled as he watched a young mum breast feed her infant. Pinkie sat down and began to pack the bubble with ash and rock. He lit the thing and toked it until the ash was through. Then he loaded it again this time for Giz, but Grandad was too mesmerized by the hippy chick to notice how much he packed his. It was as strong as he could muster but he didn't notice. He felt like offering the bird a toke on his crack pipe but decided against as he didn't know her, but she was gorgeous and had a lure on him. He was fascinate with the child as it drank and drank and drank.

"Lucky fucking bairn," Came a comment from Pinkie.

Giz sneered and got the bubble back.

Pinkie and Grandad had to pull their gaze off her and started to talk about who the band was most like.

It was a Jefferson Airplane song '*White rabbit*'. And it was pretty much flawless. Gizmo smiled his chine'ad eyes out and began to drop an eckie. He smiled and gulped a large bottle of Budweiser. The cargo was limited but they had enough to last them two maybe three hours. They had large bottles of Bud and a couple bottles of cider Merrydown (Grandad had insisted). Giz just shrugged his shoulders at his brother at the Merrydown being bagged. Pinkie smirked as they had four each of the big Budweiser's.

The woman who must have had enough wrapped her child and left. The three of them were drooling as she laughed and said, "Tough luck boys I'm married to the bass player".

Pinkie snorted a laugh then said, "No, no, nae hassle doll we was just curious as to how often your baby gets fed that way".

She smiled and replied, "As often as I'm awake and I can tell you that's morning noon and night".

Pinkie laughed and Grandad asked, "Does it hurt I mean or is it just naturally satisfying?"

She smiled and laughed, then replied "Both".

They began to laugh.

"Bye boys," she said in a husky dusky way.

"See you doll," the three of them said in unison. Then wet themselves with laughter.

Grandad carried on, "That bairn isnea gonna end up queer or weird".

She joined her man at the side of the stage and they left in a top of the range Alfa Romeo. The child was content the whole time. Never done anything other than drool. Grandad produced a bottle of Merrydown cider (Gold seal), which there were three of. One each. He began to chase the cocaine with some lovely booze. He then produced his cocaine kit that comprised of one razor a small vial and a small mirror. He lined up a line for each of them then bobbed down took his first, numbing his nose. Then he handed the mirror to Pinkie who took his toot and took it well. Then Giz who got an instant kick from the booze and the coke. He whizzed and carried on drinking his Bud. The three of them got the giggles as the buzz rushed through them.

The festival played on and people came and went. Everything from a casual to a yardie to a biker was there. Grandad knew he had to punt to them as much as he could. They became popular as people could see they were obviously the ones to see for Eckies and dust. Giz dived along to the Off-license and bought a crate of Grolsch. Then came back as the last of the product was being sold.

Giz knew that there was not a lot left so he grabbed Grandad and said, "How much you got left?"

Grandad smiled and said, "Chill out Giz, I got more at the den".

Pinkie smiled and began to roll a joint, a nice three skinner as only Pinkie could do, in his own way, which Grandad admired him for.

"A true genius," said Gramps as he stood watching Pinkie make the skins up. He lit a fag as Pinkie began to crumble the dope into the skins and cigarette, Gramps was always enthralled by the way a joint was rolled, especially when it was one of his muckers. I mean he knew that there was more than one way to skin a cat, but Pinkie he had a way. And it was always at how well it smoked. Pinkie had a knack that Grandad couldnea doubt. He still loved to watch though, especially if they were at a session where people were saying hellos and goodbyes to each other. They met and greeted and slept with the knowledge that tomorrow was another day, some people kicked their habits, others, well they still had something to prove, and carried on their ghostlike existence.

They knew most people were sociable at a field event, a festival. They were groaning and honing their skills gathering enough to pay off bills both sides of the law. It would surprise you, the number of officials that had their toes stuck in that pond. Grandad carried on swigging away the Bud he had in his hand, when out of the other end of the field Marvin, Beefy and Nichol walked over to them and sat down.

Giz smiled and handed each of them a Grolsch and Pinkie handed Gramps the meticulous and to the point joint. He toked it and handed it to Giz and the other three smiled.

"You alright Grandad?" asked Beefy.

Grandad smiled, "Aye man".

Beefy fished around and produced a bag of whizz. Grandad who was stoned as anything said, "we're alright Beefy."

Grandad smiled as a joint was handed to him. He immediately cannon balled the joint with the last of his big buds. He inhaled and held the smoke as long as he could then with a cheeky face exhaled and smiled as the smoke blew from deep in his lungs and out, he then handed the joint to Giz who was opening a Grolsch and doing exactly what Grandad had done. He could hear the band on the stage as they did a rendition of *'Brown Sugar'* by the Stones, an excellent cover at that. Grandad produced his coke kit and his bubble and went straight into rock back mode. This time he loaded off the spoon and mixed a healthy one, one that would make Jagger proud.

Beefy smiled and lay back after the joint got roached. He carried on drinking the Grolsch that Giz had passed to him. Nichol smiled a Joker toker grin and began to put the skins together for another juicy mind watering joint. This was done also with class and subtlety. He breathed on his fingers after the crumble went along the tobacco and skins. Then shaped the joint perfectly. The joint was then lit and the smoke clouded them as it gathered around them, it was fog-like and it was cool as fuck. They had their own cloud, Yep Jagger would have been proud of them. But alas that was really a pipe dream and no one mentioned it as none of them could handle the bubble bursting on them.

No, they had to come to terms (Boo Hoo) with the fact that they may never meet anyone famous. But miracles happen every day. And grandad smiled as the smoke bubbled in his crack pipe. Then he handed it to the mighty Pinkie, who was in his element. Then Marvin picked it out of Pinkies hand, who was coughing slightly from the vanilla cloud that was shaping more and more around them. Nichol passed the joint round the six of them and they carried on enjoying their high and the music. Grandad opened a bottle of Grolsch and sunk it in one gulp.

Nichol laughed as he watched gramps do it. "You know what we need and that's some talent."

Beefy laughed at this, "we could go and see some of that puntang at tipplers."

They all smiled and Grandad got hard at the thought of seeing the Go-Go dancer. He remembered when he got out the Y.O. and went drinking before Shimmey vanished. And before Liam had dropped dead and overdosed. No, those days were gone and retribution had been lain on the skulls and Paki. He smiled a bittersweet smirk and laughed as Beefy started to make jokes about a pussy whipped Grandad blowing kisses at him and rubbing his crotch and saying, "Why can't I get a girl like that?"

Then laughed and Marvin in his deepest voice said, "You aint man enough boy".

Grandad laughed as did the rest of them.

They then waited until the sun began to sink then they headed along to tipplers. They were all ripped and tripping of the crack. They went into Tipplers and, low and behold, she was there again, her lovely muff her lovey physique. She was as close to an angel they were going to get. That's when Grandad had an idea. And that idea was to go to the Sauna just up fae the Tartan Club. They all pitched in and left after giving the girl a round of applause and a whistle.

"I'm still in love wae her," said grandad as they walked towards the Massage Parlour. None of them had even thought of going to a Sauna and grandad wondered if it would be smelling of clap and crack and beer. Pinkie was designated hitter, so he buzzed the Intercom.

The voice came over smooth and silky. "Fingertips, this is Catrina here, can I help you?"

Pinkie smiled and scored one for the good guys. "Aye, er I wus wondering if me and my mates could get a massage?"

The voice went quiet then with a small laugh the woman asked, "How many is there of you and what sort of massage are you interested in?" Grandad dug Pinkies shoulder and hissed "Tell her man, tell her".

Then Pinkie smiled and said, "erotic one for each of us and that's six of us".

She went quiet then the magnetic lock buzzed and they walked up the stairs. Grandad went first. And Pinkie followed. They were on for a hell of a time, a hell of a time. And this was was just the right fix they needed for them to bond, especially Pinkie who was lost without his Pauline. They had split up soon after he got released.

"To wild for her," were the words used by Paulines mum that had devastated him, he just used more junk, more alcohol. This was just what the doctor had ordered. Giz on the other hand was out of place in this situation as he was still burning a candle for Janice.

Grandad well he just didn't give a fuck. Sheila never kept tabs on him anyway, I mean they still slept with each other and it wasn't official, but they knew each other enough to know that fidelity was not always on the menu. They got to the top of the stairs and walked through the beaded curtain. Grandad sniffed, 'Oh' he thought and the aromatic stench wasn't what he expected it was sweet and warm smelling. With what could only be described as a hint of coffee. A dark silky smell then a half-naked brunette walked by and Marvin snapped his fingers "Brunette", he said then a blond and then a red-head.

Beefy smiled and said, "All the colours under the rainbow".

Nichol laughed as they were shown into the main area where the heavenly secretary smiled, "You need to fill out this form," then she handed each of them a Piece of paper with a disclosure on them saying that lawfully they would be a paying recipient of a binding contract unto which they would waive all rights of damaging.

Beefy looked at the paper and laughed. "Aye lads their no cutting any corners".

Grandad smiled, signed his straight away. He then started to look at the women that each had a photo display that consisted of the ladies' front and naked bodies. Grandad looked through as did the other five. Grandad who was at point no return fancied a brunette. Giz settled on a blonde. Grandad snatched his paper away reading what he was intending and said, "You no had enough blondes".

Giz grinned and snatched the paper back, "Aye and no".

Grandad handed his choice over to the receptionist. She smiled and picked up the phone and said, "Angela sweetheart you're on" and a couple of minutes later in walked this stunning brunette. Not big chested but stunning with beautiful striking blue eyes. Grandad's jaw dropped as she walked towards him. The other five of them smiled and laughed.

Pinkie laughed and said, "You got your hands full with her, you want me to join you?"

Grandad gurgled and then replied, "Nah man I got it". He then went through the room that housed the masseuse and her table. She smiled and began to undress Grandad.

"So, what's your name man?"

Grandad smiled and replied, "My name is Leon, but they call me Grandad".

She then seductively pulled his trousers and reached down into his boxer shorts. Grandad's mouthed rounded into an 'OH' and she began to suck and stroke his cock.

He was going, "Steady, steady, steady". He was saying this to stop him from blowing his.

She stopped for a second and spoke, "You ready?"

He smiled and she gave it two more strokes and a gentle soft lick. He came all over her face. As he did so he gave off an almighty groan that everybody in the parlour could hear.

Pinkie was taken through to another room, he had picked a blonde.

Giz was completing a simple doggy style with her. She was crying out, "Come on fuck me baby".

Giz was not the one to shirk on his responsibilities and fucked her silly. Beefy had picked a strawberry blonde, he was mesmerised by her. But Beefy was about to show just why he worked and why they called him beef. Nichol and Marvin had each got a twin each. A blonde buxom pair. They were a pair of scousers. And Marvin and Nichols eyes widened as they watched the two of them approach them. Nichol was taken away by his hand and into a room where he found out what pleasure really was. The music that was being piped in was Depeche Mode *'Dead of Night'* "We are the dead of night. We're in the zombie room".

The music was ideal, custom made for that particular hour. Grandad was finding out more and more about why they call them Pro's. He was learning that it was woman's touch that he needed. They all finished with their women and gathered looking well, well, shell shocked, as if a pleasure bomb had gone off on the six of them. They were dishevelled yet at the same time satisfied. The smiles they wore were goofy and simple, but they would always treasure that day.

The six of them had made a pact to do that again. They paid up a total of nine hundred pound for the six of them. They walked down the stairs all of them on cloud nine. They headed back to Broomies and went to Nichol's den. Where they cheerfully sat and smoked crack and rolled joints. They were in good cheer and it had been worth every penny. Pinkie dived down the stairs to the corner shop and bought a load of Tenants lager. They got wired into their stash and cargo. They talked about how gifted the girls they had just had sex with and it wasn't long until they were pissing themselves at how loud Grandad had been.

"Man, I could not believe how gentle and sensuous she was man",

Beefy laughed and replied, "I know we all heard you groan as you came".

Grandad grinned sat back and sparked his bubble. He had a good toke of the crack pipe. Then slipped into a small dream, his cock was still tingling and he was still coming in his pants. And he didn't have to think hard about the session. She really pushed his buttons.

Beefy smiled and said, "well I went in there like an Olympics athlete".

Pinkie smiled and carried on rolling his joint. "I bet you did, I bet you did".

Gizmo smiled and drank a can of lager. "I must have fucked her every way possible. And even some way's impossible".

Marvin smiled and said, "Well mine, well she was, well gentle".

Nichol smiled and said, "Mine tae".

Grandad smiled and said, "Well now you know why they call it Fingertips Sauna." They all sat and smoked and toked all the rest of the night. Pinkie put on the CD player and played Depeche Mode's Exciter album. They made a point not to depend in themselves as they all knew they would be going back to that Parlour. But six of them decided not to tell a single soul as it was a safe bet and they had made the first moves on what had been an extraordinary and a love and secret love for the six of them. They would do that again nearer Christmas.

Grandad and Pinkie left and went to their den, where they would split their product money and invest in some more white and also eckies, They were really shinning in their own and investments, well the Mancunian connection was well bountiful. And Pinkie had re-opened his connection with Dundee and everything was flowing and people were not short of drugs or money. James sat down and started to spliff up. Grandad went and seen the beer situation. Yep, a whole load of becks nice and chilled. Grandad took one out popped the cap and sat back "I think I'm getting a hangover".

Pinkie laughed and replied, "Sure it's no baw ache?"

Grandad smiled and said, "Aye if it's no she definitely is going to be a regular thing".

Pinkie and Grandad laughed.

"Shit hot though eh?" said Pinkie.

Grandad started to spraff about the woman breastfeeding her child. Pinkie smiled and said, "I take it that's a turn on fur yae?"

Grandad nodded his head, "A fucking turn on, that my friend is full on meltdown of ecstasy and it will always be a turn on. A woman who is pregnant with child is the most horny, most natural turn on ever".

Pinkie grinned and lit up his spliff. "Any way we got to talk turkey?" he said.

Grandad walked to the kitchen scuffing his timbies as he walked to the kitchen. This was sure laziness from him, but he was never one to stand on ceremony. He popped another Becks and shouted through to Pinkie, "You want another one?"

Pinkie smiled and shouted through to the kitchen "Aye why no".

He popped a second one for Pinkie, then scuffed his way back into the living room. Pinkie took the becks and swigged it nearly draining it straight away. Gramps sat back down and smiled, "What you want to spraff about?"

Pinkie smiled and responded, "I wanna a bigger cut".

Grandad laughed out loud and replied, "You wanna a what?"

Pinkie smiled and they carried drinking "I wanna a bigger cut".

He said and Grandad shook his head, scoffed and replied. "You already got two cuts."

Pinkie snorted in indignation, "Yeah and I want a bigger piece".

"We are bringing in four times than when we first started," continued Pinkie.

Grandad smiled in a sarcastic way, "That dusnea leave a lot for you know Cha and that, and they pretty much took over as they are quality muscle mate and I ain't short changing them".

Pinkie breathed out and said, "I want out mate?"

Grandad sat up and went, "Out, you mean retire?"

Pinkie nodded his head and started to build another joint, "I aint got the legs for it anymore," he said and began to wrap the skins around the tobacco and hashish. "You know we lost two friends and two soldiers".

"Aye but that's the business we're in".

Pinkie sparked the spliff and carried on. "I know I know you think I'm a bottle merchant".

Grandad spat out, "No a fucking lunatic".

Grandad stood up and put on his jacket. "I'm awa hame. I'll speak to you in a couple of days."

He then walked out and went straight up tae his mams. "Fucking Pussy, he thinks he just commands and the deed is done. A bigger slice, wait till Becksy hears this one, he'll hit the roof".

Giz exited the stairwell of Nichols flat. And headed back to his mams, he was super fucking stoned. He noticed that Junior Coleman was visiting his family as his Subaru was parked adjacent the house that his family were in. Giz knew the Colemans and knew them well They were a family of bouncers and bar-staff. Grandad had a fight with him the second day of school, but after that they were cool. Grandad never needed to suck up and Scott respected that. They had several conversations about teachers. Who was bad and who was good. Grandad filched a bullet from his mams partner and gave it to Scott as a mark of respect. They never steely eyeballed each other or anything. Scott even asked his opinion on certain girls that he fancied. Leah Campbell being one, she was hot and her ass, well it was gorgeous, she walked with a slight wiggle and Grandad's eyes well they couldn't get enough. He was transfixed with her. Scott smiled and responded, "That's a class a girl man ken". #Grandad just nodded his head and headed away to his guidance.

CHAPTER

Giz sat in his room and thought this could'nea be any better until his window was silently chapped by Janice. Giz smiled as he knew she was welcome at his house any time she liked. He let her in quietly. She was horny and well, you know Giz had already emptied his baws. She sat on the bed and sparked a doobie. Giz smiled and whispered to himself, "Can't help the weather," then dove straight at her, necking and twisting his clothes off. Janice did the same.

'Okay' He thought. Then they settled down and began to make love. Giz was rocketing to heaven with pre climax and full-on orgasms. Janice tittered in his ear he smiled as the honey dew of cum and other liquids wrapped around their bodies and they heated up. They had no other words so the exchanged I love yous and carried on until the break of dawn. They then fell into a most relaxed sleep as they often did when they hooked up. This was well and true as neither of them had anything else to do.

Grandad spiked his bitch he was relieved to get home and inject into his bitch. His mam and her new partner. Were sound asleep. Gramps unloaded the tourniquet and pilled the pin from his bitch. The rush nearly knocking him unconscious, but he held on to the rush and neatly smiled and opened his eyes. He put on his discman and listened to The Downward Spiral by the Nine Inch Nails. He loved the whole industrial is in trouble side of it well it was very Nietzsche. You know the whole collapse of civilisation and us being run by the Umbermensch (Superman). And he didn't believe in Batman so he must be on about a race of blonde haired blue eyed geniuses. He smiled as God wasn't dead or so his mother would have you believe. Grandad smiled as the cd went the distance and he really believed that someday he would strike it rich. He just had to be cautious. Two wars he had survived and was lucky to be alive as they had lost a lot, including two close friends and handers from the Kirky Bairns. After Aleck got his neck broke, they lost all their connections through in Glasgow. It meant that they had to rely on Dundee and Manchester. They knew that they were open to another war, and they had to be careful as they weren't top of Britain. Grandad smiled, woke at about two in the afternoon.

Sheila was at the door talking to his mam. "Aye Lorna things have been quiet since the rumbles."

Sheila smiled and lit a fag, Grandad slipped on a jumper that he had just been washed. It was a heavy cotton jumper fae the Officers Club. And Tequila had bought it for him two Christmases ago. He loved it as it really kept the body warm and it was stylish. She had taste. And Grandad accepted the fact that she knew Grandad and knew what he liked.

"Awright doll?" came Gramps question. She smiled and they entered, his mam leading the way. The three of them headed into the kitchen where they sat and spraffed about how nobody had shut down a crew like that especially after them losing two boys and favour going bad. No, they had clearly won and stamped it with authority all over them. The Manchester connection (Quality Street Gang) had put the wind right up the W.H.S.C. a lot of problems were solved during the rumbles and people were wary not to cross the Y.B.C. as it appeared as if they were invulnerable.

They spoke for a good hour and Tequila was itching to get Grandad on his own. She was horny, and Grandad felt her hand stroke him under the table. Instant hard on. The conversation came to an end and Grandad went through his room with Tequilla. They began to get hot and heavy, kissing and fondling each other, she smiled as they got undressed and made love. This went on until the early hours of the morning. Then they fell asleep. Having no concern for anything else other than themselves. They were natural, they knew each other and that was a major part of the two of them, it didn't matter if they cheated on each other as they knew when they were together. That they were right for each other. They had no concerns about the green-eyed monster. No, they were completely open and honest with each other and their time was their time. Yeah, they argued, all couples argue. But jealous? No, neither of them was jealous. They held each other sacred and that was why they were going steady. He was close to putting a ring on her finger and maybe even a necklace. Grandad carried on the bad work and she carried on punting to her friends. That's just business for the two of them. They had a steady income coming in and Grandad had been careful enough not to let things surge over him and her like a tsunami. No, he had been extra careful and had the Brief and various officials continually paid off. So, he didn't have to worry about the law grabbing him and putting him on remand. He was like I said a genius when it came to money and slippery. He was an expert at getting out of jams. Him and his friends were covered. But as ever there was a storm brewing in a teacup. And Grandad knew he had been a major target for the serious crime squad and that kind of justice he could live without.

They were trying to pin a couple of murders on him and a couple of robberies. No, they had a huge hard on for him and every now and then he would notice a meat-wagon. Circling him. Sheila smiled kissed his cheek, "see I got your back". She then took him into an alley and handed him a couple bags of kit. Knowing that these fucks were staking him out, eyes and ears everywhere.

She reminded him if he had to phone use a public phone box. And even then, be cautious, "as those stinking feds carried a lot of resentment," She said then lit up as the rain began to beat down and they were off into a stairwell and up to Susan's house in the flats adjacent, Grandad's mother's flats. They sheltered and sat as Susan put on a brew. Sheila cuddled into Grandad and they sat and had a good chat about survival on the streets, Susan was fascinated by Grandad. I mean how to pop your looks and score and keep no books. She had a crush on him. He would gladly have taken her up on the offer only she looked the double of Sheila but with glasses. Grandad never tired of playing that fantasy over of them two having ahem a 'scuse my French but a cock fight. And when it happened Leon just turned over after it was over and groaned.

The two them giggled as this happened. A Grandad got a new meaning for the name Gramps. He was never ribbed so much in his puff when he went across to Toby's whose woman, a stunning brunette, listened as he took the mick out of Grandad. Moan and groan. Grandad took it and took it well. They then carried on their coke session.

"How's Jimmy?" Came the question from a rushing Gramps.

Grandad and Toby had a lot of these drug filled soirée in which neither of them could say how high.

"Jimmys good, seeing a blonde lass called Claire".

Grandad swigged on his beer and carried on the session. "He still pissed at me?"

Toby smiled. "He's over her man nae need to worry".

Grandad smiled and said, "Well he's still a mate in my eyes".

The man didn't even raise his voice when Tequilla told him she had feelings for Gramps. He took it and took it like a man. They said farewell and Jimmy wandered into a new relationship. He never had cross words with her and she knew that the two of them had been around each other so much that they never let women interfere with a friendship that had taken time to last. And they knew each other and respected each other. Often, they were shit faced and often enough they had been the centre of attention in the area. Grandad was still honourable with most of his punters. Never undercutting them and never taking their business as a sign of weakness that kind of fealty was dangerous. Grandad kept things straight and to the point, you paid or you didnea pay, either way you didn't abuse his trust and he only honoured you once if you didnea pay, you were struck of the tick list and guess what nae drugs for you. But either way you were gonna pay. Grandad kept a firm grasp on his business. And people talked like people did, saying Has hassin when he passed by the rumours about him being an assassin, well some people took it to heart, others dismissed it as legend.

Some of the older wise women crossed themselves as they knew he wasn't as innocent as some people were making him out to be.

"Just sells wacky baccy." Some said, others that it was a record as long as the guy's arm. Only Grandad knew and that was a testament to the fact that he was as much a legend as most pop stars. But he always remembered family came first. And Tequilla was practically family. Her Brother Billy knew Doughnut and knew him well. But they were staying outside the whole drugs game, I mean neither of them were that innocent. A little bit of dope and plenty of alcohol, Peave was the name in Scotland. Grandad had often just arrived just as Billy was either leaving or had just left. Grandad smiled and sat down nine times out of ten Grandad was welcome but every now and then Doughnut needed a break. And he would send Grandad away fae the door. This only happened once in a while. They sat one time and watched an Arnie marathon of movies including *Conan*, *Raw deal*, *Commando* and *Red Sonja*. Grandad columnar fault his uncle still staying away from the mundane normal way of life and living it his way. Grandad had immense respect for Doughnut, and it showed when the family got together at weddings and wakes. But all things said he had declined a normal way of life and when, his Grandad, Aleck Allan, had died Gramps was taken back when it happened. Then he heard from the Minister as he spoke about things Aleck had done, Wall of Death and various other things that bike riders did then for kicks. This included racing and showing off their latest builds. It was fashionable then and life was a hell of a lot cheaper and being as they were pretty much stuck for time, they were able to really explore the dangers of racing and motorcycles. I mean, that was and still is the whole ideology of racing and street gangs, it wasn't a new thing, but it would never tire, even now people were fascinated about bikes and muscle cars. And you've got to remember this is Britain we're talking about so the weather was well dismal and cold most of the time. But they still had meets and festivals.

CHAPTER

Giz woke with Janice curled into his chest. He smiled and she breathed softly on his body, she was soft and gentle and couldn't have been a more responsive lover. He shifted slightly and drew a fag from his half empty pack. He lit the fag and took a comforting drag. Janice had a small blissful look on her face and that said it all, he was glad to be alive. Pinkie arrived about half an hour after they woke up and the house was buzzing with activity. Pinkie let himself in, Janice and his mum were having a spraf about various things from current affairs to the word on the street. They were both pretty much clued in on both. They were having a right old chin wag.

Pinkie smiled and went and made himself a brew. He sat down and listened to the two of them nattering on. They pretty much had a fine sense of time and the two of them would laugh every now and then. Pinkie smiled at the joys to watch a couple of women get so submersed in general chit chat. It was to be applauded and never to be interrupted. Pinkie picked up the phone and dialled Grandad.

His mam answered, "Gratton House, whose calling?"

Pinkie smiled again at the snobbery and asked, "Is Leon home Mrs Gratton?"

Leon's mam smiled and said, "It's Lorna, James and I'll just go and get him". She then went through to Leons room as he was sleeping. "Leon, Leon".

He stirred slightly, "Aww Mam I was just about tae..." Then he stretched and yawned and woke up.

"Your Pal James is on the phone".

Grandad slipped his 501's on and went through to the kitchen. "Awright Pinkie?"

Pinkie smiled, "Aye man how are you?"

Grandad would have bit his head off for the suggestion that he had made the other night but Gramps was well still groggy from his night on the Raz.

"Aye I'm grand."

Pinkie smiled then did the simplest thing he could and that was apologise. "I'm sorry for putting you on the spot the other night."

Grandad relaxed, "Ach man it's just the way the cookie crumbles."

Grandad finished getting dressed after the phone call in which he explained that he was in no way responsible for the amounts that they were bringing in and it was shared as equally as it could be. But Pinkie was not satisfied, he never showed it though and decided he would wait until there was more product and more profit. But of course, he was going to have to wait until he was in a position of power. I mean he understood why he was lucky but thought he deserved more and was probably right tae. But Grandad was the man with the connections. He set up the distribution connections down Manchester and was the only man Paul trusted.

After the war was over, they realised that they had become popular with smack and dope as well as Eckies and LSD. If there was a shake down. well, the polis had been well and truly bought off and was usually someone starting off, but they hadn't paid anything into the business. Usually they got a call either from Paul or Gregg telling them they were being closed down and if they wanted to carry on punting, they had to grease the wheels. They pretty much rolled over as the polis landed on their doorstep about five minutes after the call had finished. Grandad was pleased with the non-action way Paul had handled other dealers in his patch. Paul as always was super chill.

CHAPTER

Marvin woke in the morning after the visit to the brothel and smiled and said, "I guess it wasn't a dream". Then he scratched his pubis and cock, knowing only that his loins ached and it wasn't from wanking. He smiled and lit up. His brother Kwami was away into Glasgow to run with his compadres in the West. Basically, he was going in a train journey with the Celtic boys, and he was going to get pissed and stoned. Then they would maybe invade a pub or go to a club.

Marvin smiled and got straight on the phone to Beefy. Beefy smiled as he answered the phone.

"Awright Beefy?" Asked Marvin.

Beefy toked the last of his joint and replied, "Aye man. That was pretty cool yesterday?"

Marvin smiled, "I don't know about you, but my cock is sare and I think I've ruptured one of my baws".

"Aye but it was worth it," said Beefy.

They carried on talking measuring each other's mindful capacity (how much they remembered). Marvin told Beefy that Kwami was away on a bender. They wouldn't hear from him until mid-week.

Grandad was straight on the blower to Tequila. "You wanna hook up?"

She smiled and replied, "Sure toots, when?"

Grandad smiled, "this afternoon we can have a meal delivered or maybe even go out for a sit-in meal at that Italian restaurant next tae the gay bar".

Sheila smiled and replied, "Well the restaurant sounds good, but we could easily order Pizza and roll in the hay all day and night".

Grandad laughed as she was good at getting straight to the point. He smiled, "Then come over and remember that my mam and Raymond will be around."

Sheila laughed, "Well they two can buy there ane pizza."

He hung up and told his mam that Sheila was on her way and that they were kicking back and relaxing with a takeaway.

Lorna smiled and exhaled her cigarette, "Aye son you know she's always welcome here".

Grandad went for a shower and sprayed himself with deodorant.

She was prompt and always clean living. This led her into Gramps's arms and all his charms worked out for him. She was never taken for granted and always kept herself clean. The doorbell went and Gramps answered it promptly. Tequila wrapped her arms around him and they kissed. This was a major statement that was the life of Grandad. He knew in his heart he was lucky. And his mum lit up another fag. She smiled and thought to herself 'that's my boy'.

They went straight to bed and made love. Grandad got up and spoke. "Shit. the Pizza". He then went straight to the phone and dialled Papa Joes. "Two twelve-inch Fungi and one ham and onion" They waited the better part of an hour and the munchies was hard upon them. It arrived and grandad murmured, "At last".

He then got the three pizza's, paid the tub of lard that delivered it to his door. Then went and got two plates for each of them. They sat and spraffed and Grandad went into the fridge and produced a bottle of white wine for the lady and a beer for himself. He swigged on his beer and finished his pizza. He then got out his bubble and began to put ash on the gauze and loaded it with a nice lump of crack. He smiled and gave it to the lady first. She puffed on the pipe and the smooth vanilla coloured smoke vaporised into her lungs giving her the instant all over but especially in her head rush. Days like this were to be savoured and had to be experienced to be believed. They made love that night and it was to be remembered.

He put on his Hifi Portishead, the album was *Dummy*. It let a trippy kind of atmosphere sail through the air. They made a good night of it; it wasn't their anniversary, but they were inclined to act as if it was. No, they shared a mutual love for each other and that was rare these days. Most couples didn't go' the distance but they were hard and heavy in love wae each other and could not see the clouds on the horizon.

The clouds were gathering and gathering dark and ominously. Grandad was about to be paid a visit from and old flame. And it hit him like a bolt of lightning. He was counting out his money and his mam was cleaning the stairs at the other end of the block of flats when the door was chapped. Grandad opened the door and low and behold trouble had come a knocking. It was Dawn. Grandad's jaw landed at his feet. She was back, tanned and sensuous, she looked like a million bucks. He invited her in and shut the door. Then a song all of a sudden played in his head 'Shot through the heart and you're too late you give love a bad name'.

He smiled and looked at her fine figure She was bonnie and brown. Life had come into bloom with her, but Grandad got a bad feeling with her. There must have been an alternate motive for her being here. Sure as fuck, it was the first question he would ask.

"Why are you Here Dawn?"

Dawn smiled and said, "can I hau a cup o' tea?"

He snorted and said, "Aye why no".

Then he went and put the kettle on. Grandad smiled and got the teapot and put two Tetley's in it.

"Sugar?" He asked.

"Aye two please," she replied.

He sat down and looked at her sternly. "What do yie want Dawn?"

She smiled and lit up a fag. "I finished with my lover, he and I…"

Grandad continued to look sternly at her.

"Well, we had our moment". She continued.

Grandad smiled got up and poured the tea. "I'm with someone now and it's pretty serious".

She sighed and said, "Thought so".

Gramps let the tea stew, then after a minute or so he poured her and himself a mug of sweet tea. They spoke but Grandad was serious and wasn't letting her back into his life. The first time was bad enough. It wasn't a nightmare situation. It was well over and he knew if things could be different, he would take her back. But him and Sheila had been together a while now and it was pretty much and cheating, nah fuck that, the arguments, the lying, the out and out difficulties that sprung up with the situation. No, he respected Tequila too much. They had come a long way and it was a natural love, no overblown expectations they were just steady. And they liked and respected each other too much.

"You know you got some nerve showing up out of the blue," he said.

She sighed again.

"Things are different now, I'm pretty much set with Sheila".

She wasn't going to let it go that easily. "We could be careful and have a fling," she said and then sipped her tea.

Grandad shook his head, "Nah doll Nah," He then lit up a fag. "I respect Tequila too much to complicate the relationship".

Dawn smiled a sad lonely smile as if all her hopes had been pinned on him and her getting back together. Grandad reached across and put his hand on top of hers and said, "I'm sorry Doll but couldnea bear it if things went south again".

She smiled and drained her cup, got up and left. Grandad saw her oot. He then smiled. "she is still hot though" he said after the door shut and she walked away.

CHAPTER

Pinkie smiled and blew the rocks of his joint. He began to roach the thing. I mean long full-on tokes. He also smiled through his eyeballs and drained a Becks. The lager was like nectar to him. And he thought 'Must get in contact wae Becksy'. He then picked up the phone, his eyes slanted like a Chinaman's and he was well-munted and nothing was going to change that.

"Awright Becksy?" He asked.

Becksy smiled and replied, "Aye man sound".

Pinkie gaze was strange and stoned.

"You holding?" Asked Pinkie.

Becksy laughed, "I've got some white coming when my brother gets back".

Pinkie laughed, "You and your brother keep the punters happy."

Becksy snorted a small laugh as if the question was redundant.

"How much you selling it for?" Asked Pinkie,

Becksy smiled, knowing that the two of them were close real close, "Well the going rate on this white is sixty a gramme".

Pinkie smiled and Becksy continued. "But you get mates rates, thirty a gramme".

Pinkie smiled knowing that only Becksy's mates got a discount.

"Phone me when you get the gear,"

Becksy laughed and they hung up.

Pinkie had a good feeling about that day. It was sunny outside and Pinkie was in the mood for sunshine music. Finley Quaye's *Maverick a Strike* went on.

He sailed away on his high, the music got him in the spirit of summer. "Quicker than a Wing Chun fighting rasta is higher" came through the stereo. He loved that album he was the next best thing to Bob Marley. And that was a statement in itself. He smiled and lit up another joint savouring the quality 'grade A' cannabis. It was rocky and lovely gear he hadn't been able to score much in the jail but along came his parole and he was set free. As was Nichol and Becksy.

"Someone got paid," he said with a smile.

When he and his compadre's got back to Broomie a party and I mean a party rocked the whole west side of Edinburgh. They were fucking, smoking, drinking and generally getting shit faced, Bongs, Yodas, bottles of beers and of course girls, girls, girls. Heroes they were and hard rocking and hard toking. Grandad smiled soon as he saw Pinkie. The air was buzzing with smoke clouding over the area of broomie. Nessy was building joins three four at a time. Pinkie was given the Lions share and everybody had a good time.

Anyway, Pinkie carried on with the mellow vibe of Finley Quaye. "Even after all" Was sailing through the house. He smiled and rolled another spliff. "The murdering that go on" The stereo blasted out. There was a knock at the door. Pinkie practically floated to the door. It was Ali Grey. He was stood there grinning, he had purposes on his mind and needed to share them with Pinkie. Pinkie let him in, started into the fridge for a couple of beers, him and his amigo. Ali was smiling as Pinkie popped his Becks and swigged the thing down, it was cold and refreshing Ali let out a huge "Aaaahhhh that hit the spot" As he consumed the bottle straight away.

Pinkie smiled and produced a rather large lump of dope. Enough to keep them going. Ali smiled as Pinkie began to skin up, "How's Grandad?" came the next question from Ali.

Pinkie smiled and began to crumble the dope into his joint, savouring the smell of the dope and he answered, "Yeah, he is good Ali. How you want him for anything in particular?"

Ali produced a bag full of eckies from out his coat pocket. Pinkie nearly choked at the amount, knowing that it was one of those things that the big bag was always full and as always, they had the punter in the palm of their hand. I mean Liam when he was alive had often bragged about the quantity that was around him down south. He smiled and said, "They know how to treat a dope fiend down there. As everybody was holding. And they shared their wealth".

Ali smiled and took out five Eckies and laid them on Pinkies dope tray. They were Fioris and well they weren't bad. The rush of them was subtle but it was a kick none the less. Pinkie handed him the spliff and smashed an eckie and snorted the fucking thing. He waited a total of five minutes before the Ecstasy done what it was supposed to do.

He lay back on his couch kicked his feet up and relaxed whilst the eckie made him feel loved up. He picked up the phone and dialled Jordan's number seeing as she was only available when Pinkie needed to empty his baws.

She picked up after about three or four rings, "Maclaren residence, who's calling?"

Pinkie smiled and thought Jackpot, "Awright Jordan fancy coming to mine?"

She smiled and said, "Pinkie how are you dain? Long time no see".

Pinkie smiled and said, "I got dope and beer and Ali is here with a bag full of Eckies."

Jordan smiled "You want me tae get Angie, Hazel and Shirley?" Pinkie smiled as the blood was pumping in his veins and he was getting cool, cool rushes. They weren't the most powerful of Ecstasy but they were damn good "Aye doll get them all and bring Cargo".

CHAPTER 6

Grandad was oblivious to the party that was starting in Pinkies den he sat and smiled whilst Tequila rolled a nice joint. He kissed her as she handed him the doobie and said, "I had a visitor the other day".

She smiled and said "Who?"

Gramps took a couple of tokes fae the doobie and decided he better tell her. So, he began to tell her about Dawn arriving at his door.

She was not amused, "When was this like?"

Grandad knew when he had annoyed Tequila and she was pissed at him.

"Why didn't you tell me when this happened?"

Grandad looked at her with the biggest puppy eyes and said, "I did'nea hau a clue she was coming until she knocked on the door".

Tequilla looked at him sternly, "Did you shag her?"

Grandad sniffed and replied, "No, fuck no, I made her a cup of tea, then sent her packing," Grandad handed the joint back to Tequilla knowing she needed to calm down.

"Well don't get any ideas about going behind my back".

Grandad smiled, "Lets haw a couple o' lines of sweet toot?"

She smiled, "You never cease to amaze me,"

She said then took a couple of tokes. Grandad smiled and produced his cocaine kit and spooned some out on the small mirror. Then chop he went with the small razor blade. Then lined up two small but fat lines for them. They started to get together again, smiled as she had him like putty in her hand. And it was never a dull moment in the house with Grandad. Sheila and himself wrapped each other around their fingers. Yep, it was still summer and they had about three more weeks of sunshine. Grandad and Tequila rested that day and night. He smiled as he heard his mum locking the door and saying, "goodnight you two".

Grandad smiled as she walked back down the hall "Night mum" She smiled and went into her room and got ready for her bed.

⚜

Meanwhile Pinkie and Ali Grey were living it large hooching with pussy, the house was and both Pinkie and Ali Grey were having a ball. But without the biscuit, Becksy smiled as he rounded the corner of the Sighthill shops where when they were at High School they bought their fags and skins for their dope. He could see the flat was bouncing with birds and lads fae Broomie. Becksy smiled and said to himself, "Just in time". Then he walked directly to the party and pick up two hundred pounds, for passing go. He smiled as the usual faces and a few of the other crew were there. He smiled and sailed straight in. Free parking. He went and gripped wrists with Pinkie and looked around, they were doing buckets, they were doing shotgun blowbacks and handstand blowbacks. Tardises, which are spinning blowbacks.

There was all manner of munchies from hot dogs tae micro-chips. Banjo was there with Wolfie and Buchan. Even Davey Moss was there. Becksy was scoping out the Pun Tang. And there was a tonne of them smiling and showing each other their nails.

Becksy smiled and said tae Pinkie, "where is Gramps?"

Pinkie smiled and handed him a joint and said, "ach we felt that him and Tequila were needing a break".

Becksy smiled and nodded his head saying, "it's a shame he would have loved this soirée." Giz on the other hand was settling to a nice cosy night wae Janice. They called an Indian and poured each other a glass of wine or two. Giz and Janice were in the right place for them. Giz's Mum and Dad had silently disappeared leaving Giz and Janice to their devices. Giz made the most of it as did Janice. Grandad phoned Giz just as he was about put on another movie. He was in the mood for a horror and there were only two horrors that shocked everyone and that was *Hellraiser, One* and *Two*.

Giz lifted the phone out the cradle and Janice smiled. "It's Gramps".

He then spoke, "Gramps my main man, watcha you up tae?"

Grandad laughed as Tequila showed her leg at Gramps then wrapped the sheet around her body. "I'm... I'll phone yae back".

Giz giggled and said, "I'll no hud my breath though. Clearly you are having a ball".

He then sat down and resumed the movie. They were both engrossed in the Kirsty character who was obviously the princess who had bit off more than she could chew.

"Come on Snow White take your best shot". Came the twisted stepmom.

Giz was comfortable and Jance was averting her eyes every now and then. Particularly at the Cenobites. Especially the one who had open surgery on its throat. She was the creepiest. Well, Giz and Janice thought so.

I mean Pinhead he was sinister, but he was too rigid but that just made the film that bit more creepy.

"We have such sights to show you," then a little while later he said, "We'll tear your soul apart".

They carried on watching films until the early hours in the morning. They fell asleep on the sofa. Giz was smiling and made the connection between Boz and Pinhead. Yep, two peas in a pod. Giz woke the next morning to the door opening onto the street and someone coming in, it was Pinkie and he was on cloud nine. He had, had a roaring time full o' e's and smoke and beer. The rushes had not settled totally yet and he was major league buzzing. Giz got up and went straight to the fags.

Pinkie smiled and lit one himself and said, "You okay wee brother?"

Giz rifted and replied, "Aye man. Was it a decent party".

Pinkie's face broke into a huge grin and he was suddenly tripping again. "Aye it was braw".

Giz woke Janice up, "Hey sweetheart I got a cup of tea fir yae". She opened her eyes and then sat up and took the mug of tea which was both milky and strong at the same time.

"Perfect," She said then lit up, drank the brew and got ready to leave.

The day was new and the feelings bloomed especially with Jan and Giz. Grandad woke hearing his mother hum along tae a tune, it was a Rod Stewart tune, *Baby Jane*. Grandad fished into his jacket and produced the wee cocaine kit and started to chop a line for himself (Racking up they call it). Tequilla was in a deep beautiful sleep one in which she was really relaxed and she knew nothing could touch her as Grandad had proved time and time again that you didnea mess wae him. Especially whilst in the folds O' the Y.B.C. He was important in this junk land wasteland. He had done everything that needed to be done to keep him and his compadre's in the graces of the Cocaine Lords and Poppy lords. The rest, well the rest was a bonus but still he never took anything for granted, as the streets could be your friend one day and the next a sinister assassin. But things were smooth and plain sailing just then. And business was booming. He smiled and scratched the back of his head. Then he felt the cocaine buzz, possibly the best wake up regime you could get. And he did it at least three four times a day, and that was a normal day. He had little else to do and well, it was better than praying for the rain on a roasting hot day.

Grandad looked at her the Queen of hearts herself and thought life when it comes round to your turn, to bat well even if you aren't a major hitter, you got to stay sane. And she was the treasure that he held dear. He smiled flicked the ash off his fag and watched her some more. She began to stir. A waking queen. He sat and counted his blessings.

She smiled and said, "Leon no like you tae hover, get under these covers".

He did just that and she wrapped her arms around him and said the word "Lover". They began to giggle and tussle about they were extremely in love and nothing was going to change that.

Dawn sat at home in a sullen sad mood she was hoping for a better result with Grandad but alas she sobbed gently over her cup of tea. I mean what did she expect she had dumped him in the first place. And he was inside, so it must have been even more difficult for him. Anyway, she thought, things change, feelings change and nothing was a certainty especially in the drug world. It was full of challenges. And unfortunately, one of them was keeping a relationship. She sighed a small lovesick sigh. Then carried on drinking her tea. It was just one of those things that you had little or no control over.

CHAPTER 7

Grandad rolled up a wad of notes, all profit. He still had the house up in Rosehearty and hoped to return there soon. He was just making sure everything was running smoothly down south and that the Dundee connection wasn't interfering with the Manchester one. When it came down to it both connections were good earners. Grandad smiled as the fag drooped from his lips. It was still grating on him that Pinkie wanted a bigger share.

"Cheeky bastard," he said out loud as he rolled up a chunk of change. He didn't expect that to come fae Pinkie. And thought how different the two of them had turned out to be. Pinkie had been loyal, even the time he had done was priceless. Grandad took a draw of his fag, flicked the ash and carried on counting the money. He was being vigilant with the connections, but he knew he needed to be as well, well it was a tricky business and grandad was seasoned, a very experienced dealer. The streets were awash wae drugs.

The Phone rang and Gramps answered "Hello".

Pinkie smiled on the other end of the line, "Awright Gramps?"

Grandad smiled and replied, "Aye man no bad, what you up tae?"

Pinkie smiled and said, "Och I was just wondering, did you think any more about the money situation and whether it was feasible for me to get a larger slice?"

Grandad thought again 'Cheeky Bastard!' Then he replied. "No James I got to take it up with the rest of the crew."

Pinkie sighed down the phone as if this was hassle he did'nea need. But Grandad was adamant and was sure as well that the fucker was at it. Grandad was two seconds away from biting the fuckers head off. But he calmed himself down counted to ten and carried on the conversation. Explaining to Pinkie that it was a team effort and everybody got paid. And well the slice was the slice. They hung up and Grandad muttered "Prick" then carried on counting out the money. The profit he had made wasn't much but enough to see him and his mother right. He was well, was very pissed. And the baws on Pinkie, he thought well if this doesn't cause an argument then nothing will. He snorted a half laugh and then trapsed off to his uncle's. To secure some of his profit in a bank account that he had procured in his cousin's name.

"It's getting to be a tidy sum Leon," said Doughnut.

Grandad smiled and replied, "it's my rainy-day money".

Doughnut smiled and said, "You still got that Pistol?"

Grandad laughed and replied, "Yep".

Doughnut nodded his head in amusement, "How's Tequilla?"

Grandad smiled and said, "She's grand mate, grand".

Doughnut counted the money quicky then shouted to Debbie. "Debbie".

She came running, "Aye da?"

Doughnut smiled and grandad nodded his head.

Doughnut spoke to Debbie, "You going along tae the shop?"

She smiled and replied, "Aye da",

"Well will you dive into the bank and put this in wee David's account?"

She took the money and then went and fetched the bank book. She put on her coat then went and did the shopping for the house. Doughnut smiled and offered Grandad a bottle of Smirnoff Moscow mule.

Grandad clicked his lighter shut right after lighting a fag and said, "Aye why no".

They sat and shot the breeze talking mainly about what sort of society they lived in these days. Grandad was talking about how if the criminal element in the drug game was given the rights to sell drugs the world would be a hell of a lot kinder. People like Liam wouldn't overdose, Shimmey wouldn't be murdered. Grandad was, well putting forward a complete Idealistic case, a utopia, a perfect world. Maybe the suffering would stop. Maybe we would have the resources to cure every ailment. They spoke for what was the better part of a day.

Doughnut was thinking he was making a strong argument in the world could be cured sense. But what if it didnea work, what if it left the world with a race of zombies. I mean brain dead animalistic shambling zombies, just wanting more, and more narcotics. How would we stop the constant appetite that is narcotics. Addiction services would be swamped the world would be left going cold turkey. Sweating groaning dying of its own desires.

No, the two them were bang on and the subject was fascinating to the both of them. They were pretty drunk when grandad really put forward the question "What if…" They two of them raised the questions and argued but not in an aggressive way. It was general consensus that all drugs should be legalized then the sinister part of society would be able to be treated. Doughnut finished of seeing the clarity of wisdom from his nephew.

"Huh," he said.

Then Grandad turned and said, "anyway fuck all that lets get shit faced".

They then began to tan a whole crate of Moscow mules. It was one of those things that neither of them was backing down. So, it was a stalemate. And they were just getting sozzled. Doughnut then put on *'Scarface'* and they watched it the two of them engrossed in the film.

⚜

Giz smiled and reached over for his cuppa that Janice had made him, he was totally engrossed in the telly they were watching Alan Parkers *The Wall* Pink Floyd. Janice was sat with an emery board and was smoothing the nails that she had just painted. She was an expert on all things cosmetic and often wondered if she could pull enough capital, she would be able to open her own beauty parlour. This was alas a dream she had and never managed to pull enough money together. Really, she didn't know where to start. It was a distant and somehow impossible dream. But she was always living, in hope she got the college studies and went as often as she could, but she realised that it was more than she thought. She needed to do her own accounts and managing the store required a degree in business management. It was a whole mountain to climb and she didn't know how to start. She carried on doing her nails. Giz sipped his tea. *The Wall* came to an end and she smiled and looked at Giz, "I'm bored".

Giz bust out a laugh, "I bet you are".

She smiled and put down the nail board. "You wanna step out wie me?"

Giz started to set the skins up for a nice three skinner. He thought 'Maybe it would be nice to go out on the razz'. He shrugged his shoulder and said, "where you wanna go toots?"

She thought for a minute or two then came up with an answer, "The Rocking Horse".

Giz licked and began to wrap the joint into shape. "Yeah, why not," he said, then bit the wick and lit the spliff. "What time is it?" he asked as the joint blazed away.

"Half past seven in the PM," she answered. "We got plenty of time it doesn't close its doors till midnight".

Giz smiled and handed her the joint, "Aye why not," he said then went and took a piss. Janice screamed in delight and went and got her party stuff. The trousers were skintight and black. She also put on a halter top, you know a boob tube, then she put on her heels and started to hum an Alice in Chains song *Rooster*.

Giz went and shaved and combed his hair. Then phoned a taxi for Nine o'clock. They sat and waited then the taxi arrived and Janice and Giz got in, Giz was wearing a Fred Perry white coat, a classic. He smiled as he got in the taxi. The driver smiled as Janice hung on Giz's arm.

"Where to mate?"

Giz smiled and said, "The Grassmarket mate, to the Rocking Horse".

The driver smiled and replied, "Yes sir, we'll no be too long".

Giz smiled and rubbed Janice's hand. A small gesture of pleasure.

She smiled and said, "My loving man".

They arrived and Giz tipped the driver for being exemplary and making it a nice smooth ride. The taxi driver handed him a card with his number on it. "Phone any time I'll be free".

Giz waved the gentleman adios and the headed into the club that comprised of three levels, the one at the top in which they entered was a small bar the second was a heavy metal disco and the basement was Indie Rock and Hip Hop. They went into the bar first and ordered a couple of jugs, one lager the other sex in the beach. Giz smiled and sat and filled a pint glass with lager. Janice smiled at him and poured some of her cocktail into a glass.

"Thanks, sweety," she said and took a good drink of her liquid refreshment. The club was just getting started and the students of the area were coming and going. Some Hippy'ish others traditional rockers. Both complemented each other. Giz put his hand in his pocket and made sure he had two things. One was his blade the other was a roll of twenties. About three to four hundred pounds worth. He also had two bags of hash one grass, the other was a rock of cocaine. About two grammes worth. They had another Jug each then went down to dance in the rock level it was playing Nirvana and then it played Stone Temple Pilots. Them some Nine Inch Nails, *Hurt* was the tune Janice screamed as the tune played away. 'You can have it all, My empire of dirt' the song played on and Giz was wondering how he had landed so lucky. And she came across after dancing to the tune and said, "Come on Giz".

Giz got up smiling and *Ring finger* was playing next. They held onto each other. He smiled and put his hands onto her perfect bum. She had her arms on his shoulders and was mouthing the song as it played on. They then went to a small table in the corner and Giz pulled out his cocaine kit and racked up a line for each of them.

Then the club started filling up and Giz buzzed out to the tunes by Metallica, Guns and Roses, Janes Addiction and Alice in Chains.

It was a good night and nobody hassled them. They were perfect for each other and nothing could happen to make them unhappy. They phoned the taxi as the club was emptying and the same guy picked them up just like he said. Everybody and their auntie were trying to get a taxi. But that was why he had told Giz to phone. Giz opened the door and him and Janice headed back to her house. They were kissing and fondling each other, nothing heavy, a small light petting session. Just enough to keep them in the mood. The walked up the stairs and into Jan's flat, where they made sweet love the rest of the night then slept until way past noon.

CHAPTER 8

Grandad was in his house having a shower and singing *Road House Blues* by The Doors. He was still a big fan and he knew that their music was timeless it would always be there. His mum rapped on the bathroom door and said, "Lunch Laddie".

Grandad dried himself and pulled on a pair of Peppe Jeans and pulled on a Luke T-shirt that cost him an arm and a leg. But it was worth it. He walked into the kitchen and sat and said, "I needed that, this heat is killing me".

His mother handed him a roll with prawn mayonnaise on it.

"Cheers mam," he said then wolfed it down in two bites.

His mam looked at him he said, "Mmmm I'm fucking starving mm". Then he finished the roll and got himself a cold frosty Becks. He began to savour the beer the amber liquid fuelling his week of drugs and hardcore living getting him right to where he wanted, he smiled and closed his eyes and said "Nirvana" then he continued to drink his beer.

The weather was roasting, it was in the twenties and baking everyone. He put on his jacket that was a light Levis denim jacket. It wasn't the most expensive jacket but was light and easy to wear. He then headed to Pinkies and rapped on the door, He was still fuming at the guy, as the idea of him getting a bigger share, well it wusnea going tae happen. He waited and Pinkie came to the door, "You okay Gramps?"

Grandad relaxed and made a small gesture as if to say, 'Could be better, could be worse' he followed through with an "Ehh".

Pinkie produced a spliff and they were about to blast off.

"Where's Giz" asked Grandad as he toked the joint.

"Oh, him and Janice stepped out last night".

Grandad smiled, "They could have waited".

Pinkie smiled and replied, "Ach leave them they're loved up".

Grandad shook his head and replied, "I know that, but her and Sheila are sisters".

Pinkie went and pushed both arms out and said whilst the joint drooped in his lips, "So".

Grandad looked at him and said, "I'm just saying it would be nice to have been offered?"

Pinkie laughed out a horse laugh, "I know, just don't take it personally".

Grandad reached for his fags and lit one, "Anyway we would just get on his nerves. He's a fussy bastard after all".

Grandad nodded his head and sparked up, "Yes I know yes I know". he said. Smiled then laughed a little. Grandad could'nea argue any more. He asked the question that was frequented by his lips, "are you holding?"

Pinkie looked at him and said, "Of course, is a pigs arse pork?"

Grandad laughed at that saying. "Watcha got?" he asked.

"Watcha need?" Came the reply.

Grandad was really in the mood for a couple of acid tabs. As they day was nice and he felt like rambling. "Got any Acid?"

Pinkie smiled and replied, "Aye I got acid, I got Jaggers and I got green microdots."

"How much?"

"How many do you want?" Replied Pinkie.

Grandad shook his head and smiled and said, "Well I like those green Dots. It is the flint ones I'm assuming?"

Pinkie smiled and said, "Aye it's the flint ones".

Grandad felt at the large roll of money in his pocket, "I'll gie you a tenner each for two microdots and a fiver each for two lips".

Pinkie nodded and produced the gear. It was a bargain as Grandad well knew. The Microdots were anywhere up to twenty a pop. Grandad counted the money and Pinkie went and got his stash. He smiled and Grandad paid him.

"You wanna trip wae me?" He asked Pinkie.

Pinkie smiled and replied. "Aye man".

Grandad dropped one of the dots. Pinkie followed suit. They sat down on his step and started tae spraff. "We'll need more fags coz this is gonna be a long, delightful night."

Pinkie handed Gramps twenty Regal and said, "We'll pick up more later at the time we peak".

Just as they were about to ramble on, they saw Giz with his coat over his shoulder and looking very satisfied, Grandad looked at him and said to Pinkie. "Look at him eh. Not a care in the world".

Pinkie laughed and took a drag of, of his fag, "Aye talk about the cats got the cream," Pinkie returned.

Grandad let of a shrill whistle as Gizmo came closer. Gizmo returned the greeting by holding up his hand and shouted, "Awright lads what's happening?"

Then he got closer and Pinkie said, "Still loved up a see?"

Giz went, "Aye and my stone didnea turn sour or anything".

Grandad took out his packet of cigs and gave one tae him.

Giz laughed, "That woman," he said and lit up, "She is something."

Pinkie stood on his doubt and said, "I take it you'll be needing a crash".

Giz laughed and replied, "Aye man".

Then went into the house, "See ya the morrow".

Gramps and himself sauntered off in search of trippy places as the acid was just about to kick in. Giz was asleep before they left the street. Gramps smiled as the warm loved up tummy rush was beginning. He loved that trippy feeling.

Pinkie went, "I'm right behind you Grandad".

The acid was nice and mellow and they had begun to see the hallucinations, certain walls were crawling and the buzz, the buzz was fucking fantastic. Grandad started to notice the birds were making tracers and he was watching the pavement crawl and slither. It was a good trip and they still had most of the night to come. The neon wilderness was leaving a nice gleam. The star glares and everything was pristine pure and well, well, you couldn't get a nicer feeling.

Pinkie smiled at one time and said tae Gramps, "Pauline disnea ken what she is missing".

Grandad sucked on a bon bon, a toffee one and was savouring the sugar attack he was having. He was so engrossed in the feeling of toffee and sugar melting into his mouth that he missed the whole speech by Pinkie about Pauline. They carried on rambling on. And getting closer and closer to peaking. Grandad produced one of the Jaggers and dropped it. It would take a while and Gramps was skilled at dropping knowing how long it takes for certain acid to gleam and when they peeked and rushed to the end of the Jagger would kick in as it takes a while for Jaggers to kick in. They headed deep into the neon jungle that was Wester Hailes.

Grandad turned and said, "Let's go tae Tequilas?" Pinkie smiled and they went the short distance tae Sheila's. The night had settled in and it was warm and easy to see why tripping was so popular, Grandad knocked on Tequilas door. She came to the door in a Next sweater and Peppe female jeans. These Jeans accentuated her bum. Grandad smiled as he couldn't take his eyes of her bum as she led them in.

Grandad smiled and said, "Want an Acid?"

She sat down and Gramps produced another bon, bon. Put the sweet in his mouth and again a sugar attack. She smiled and continued with her joint rolling. "Aye Darling what kind of acid is it?"

Gramps smiled and Pinkie spoke up and said, "Well you can hae either a microdot or a Jagger".

She smiled ripped the wick of her joint and lit it up. "A fuck it", she said then continued, "I'll hae one of each".

Pinkie produced two bags one with the bullets the other the tabs. He took one of each and handed them to her.

"You look gorgeous darling". Said Gramps. And she did. The double acid just setting her off, she looked like an angel her soft white skin her dark flaming hair bouncing as she shrugged it and laughed. Nothing could destroy that moment and if it did, he would just drop another acid and build it up again. She handed the joint to Pinkie who was obviously oblivious to the fact that she was an angel sent straight from heaven. It was the middle of summer and her freckles were showing more. As redhead's were prone to sunlight setting off their skin. Then the wallpaper began to crawl and even pinkie noticed the trippy wallpaper. She sat there and looked at the two of them, obviously engrossed in their buzz. She had a small, satisfied smile on her face and said, "Boys, boys, boys" she began to gleam of, of her two that she had dropped.

But Grandad and Pinkie were way ahead of her. Their trip was smooth and just right. And Grandad was having good one. She smiled and went through the kitchen to make herself a coffee. Grandad produced another bon, bon.

Pinkie who was totally engrossed watching the wall smiled and said, "fuck sake, these are good trips".

Grandad smiled a tripped out goofy smile, and said, "Aye man Totally worth it". He then produced another toffee bon, bon and popped it in his mouth. He was still having a good trip, and it was just right. The crawling of the wall. The smooth sugar taste. It was paradise and Gramps was in his element.

Tequila came through from the kitchen. With a mug of coffee for each of them. They each sipped but their eyes couldn't be peeled of the sitting room wall. She smiled finished her coffee and waited for the two tabs of acid to gleam. Grandad shifted his eyes back onto Tequila and smiled. They then decided to leave as they were just about to peak. Tequila said goodbye to the two of them and they started to walk tae Becksy's house. The neon wilderness was treating them well nothing to trippy but then again nothing boring.

Becksy answered the door, "Awright Pinkie? Awright Grandad?"

They both nodded at him. "What are the pair of you on?"

Grandad smiled and nudged Pinkie. "Gie the man a lay on".

Becksy smiled, "I've got poppy," he said.

Pinkie smiled again and said, "Aye I've got Acid. Dots and Jaggers".

Becksy smiled and replied, "How much?".

Pinkie replied, "Ten a dot and five a Jagger".

Becksy smiled and produced a ten- and five-pound note. "I'll hau one of each".

Grandad smiled his eyes out, "We're aboot tae peak so…"

Becksy dropped both and laughed. "Well judging by you two, they are obviously decent acid".

Grandad shook his head with a satisfied smile on his face. Pinkie smiled "Where are we of to next?"

Gramps lit a fag and replied, "Let's go tae the den".

They said goodbye to Becksy and headed towards their flat at Sighthill. They got in and started straight away to build a joint.

"You wanna call a few party girls?" Asked Pinkie.

Grandad smiled and said, "Aye why not".

Pinkie smiled back and replied, "Who Angie, who?"

Grandad smiled, "Jordan". He said then reached for the phone.

Fifteen minutes later Jordan arrived and Pinkie let her in. Trapsing with her was Angie and Vicky Gregg. The buzz was still going. They put on some music and that was Jimi Hendrix, the album *Electric Ladyland*. Quite possibly the best album by the guy. Especially *Voodoo Child* it got all of them rocking and smoking and fucking. The girls weren't shy and knew they were in for a wild ride. Pinkie sold most of his stash that night and his pocket was fat, I mean fat. The fucking party lasted two days with no sign of a come down for either of them. Everybody else smiled through their teeth and gleamed. The pristine buzz was a welcome one. And the money well they would just invest in more product. They had a ball and knew that they had just the right amount to see them through.

Grandad had never been so munted in years and it was going to stay that way for a number of days. They finally came down and Grandad smiled and said, "I better go and see what kind of damage we've done".

Knowing that they had just punted tae half of Broomie and about a quarter of Wester Hailes. They were fucking popular. Acid like the ones Pinkie had well they were the best you could get, Pinkie was liking the money situation, and Grandad who had emptied his balls several times wanted to crash out and sleep. He got back to his mum's house with a gleam in his eye as if to say, 'thank fuck I'm me' He then went through his room sat down in his bed and lit one up. Grandad smiled and thought 'I wonder how long Sheila got out of her trip' Grandad carried on smoking then produced a bottle of Valium took a few and slept.

Giz wandered up to Janices, he was floating on air and couldn't be perturbed by anything. He arrived at her door smiling a cocaine smile. And it was priceless. He chapped on her door and waited for her to answer.

"That's my lover," she said as she opened the door. The music in the background was, *Playing with lightning* from the film Blade. And it was one of those songs that really stuck, 'Oooh I got struck by lightning' came the lyrics and Giz smiled and entered her flat. Again, that Perfume. It was so seductive and Giz couldn't think of any place he would want to be other than with her.

He smiled and asked, "What Eckies you got darlin?"

She smiled, "well I got some Hearts, I got some Mitsubishes, some fioris, and as usual Rhubarb and Custards."

Giz smiled sat down and said, "I'll Hau one of each".

Janice smiled, went through to her stash and rummaged for a minute or two. She came back with a baggie with his request in it. She smiled, put her feet up and said, "That was a good night the other night".

Giz smiled took a toot of coke and replied, "Yeah, yeah it was pretty decent". Giz rolled a joint. And his brain was watering as the smoke mixed nicely into his lungs and blood.

Janice smiled and said, "Fancy a beer Toots?".

This was a regular thing with Janice, beer and dope. She had an abundance of the stuff. And she kept the fridge filled with beer for Giz and for Giz only. He was privileged. And that was a fact, but he had genuine feelings for her, yep, he was loved up. And to him it was very real and very beautiful. She then, after handing him the Coors, sat down and said to him, "blow job, lover?"

He nearly choked on the liquid refreshment. She smiled, she loved Giz and Giz felt the same way about her he had one hell of a passionate affair with her. And she never strayed from him. I mean he took it easy and carried on with the sexual intercourse and she was really, really, good. And it wasn't just her good looks. No, she was a trickster, she could do sexual tricks, like put the condom on with her mouth. She could turn mid coitus, and blow jobs, well she was an expert. She enjoyed the giving the pleasure, but Giz was well, he was a delicate lover with an easy touch. He was slow and made sure she was satisfied with at least one orgasm. But nine times out of ten she would have several orgasms each one crashing into her like waves of the sea. It came natural to Giz and ever since she recuperated, she was Giz's and his only. He smiled and looked up at the ceiling whilst she gave him his countless blow jobs. He was in heaven and it was truly a miracle that they two were together.

CHAPTER 9

Grandad phoned Tequila and the phone rung and rung before she answered out of breath. He smiled and asked, "Tequila is everything okay?"

She smiled, "Yes Leon just self-satisfying myself". At the point she pushed the vibrator onto the phone.

He instantly got a hard on. "Okay doll I get the picture".

She smiled and rubbed the dildo onto her vagina, "Mmmmmm," She moaned "well hurry the fuck up before I go off the boil".

He grabbed his jacket and grabbed his fags then headed straight to her house. I mean Olympic runners couldn't get there any quicker. Grandad knocked on her door. And she answered with a jumper on and nothing on her legs. He grabbed her instantly and they began to neck, kiss and rub each other up. They had all the time in the world. And Sheila stuck on some Depeche Mode. *Violator* the album, was perfect for the way they were feeling. They started to fuck and it was heaven to them. After a few climaxes they sat and had a couple of J's the gear that Grandad had was soft black gold seal. And they spent the better part of a day and night having sex and getting stoned.

Pinkie sat and counted out the profit for the Acid he had and had panned out. It was a long time since he panned out. But still he was stewing in his own temper thinking he could do with settling his slice with Grandad. But he knew that Grandad if he could would give him an extra slice. He went over to the Hifi and put on Pearl Jam. The album *Versus*.

He sat back and smoked his dooberon and relaxed he had done the same as Gramps and that was cop a few vallies to bring himself down gently. The tarrie helped but Pinkie liked a vallie rush just like everyone else at the end of a trip. Becksy smiled as he took some jellies to help him sleep off the trips. He needed something that little bit stronger. And jellies were the ones that he preferred.

He was just dozing off when his mother came through, "There is a lad at the door for you,"

Becksy growled, "Who is it mam and can it no wait?"

She smiled as Becksy thought, 'Can't fault the weather'.

He got up and walked to the door, it was Polland fae Manchester. Becksy met him once before at a party at Janices. He had come up to see Grandad and he stayed for a few days.

"Awright Mate?" Asked Polland.

Becksy replied, "Aye man what are you dain in this neck of the woods?"

Polland smiled, "I got some news and it aint pretty".

Becksy had a feeling that something was rotten. "What news?" he asked then ushered Polland into his house.

The house was spotless and pristine. He went through the kitchen and Polland followed. Becksy reached into the fridge and produced two Budweiser's. They popped the cap on their beer and began to drink.

"Well?" Said Becksy.

Polland smiled and said, "someone has dobbed us all in. The serious crime squad and the CID are making connections and coming up trumps we got four weeks left before they shut us all down".

Becksy sat forward and said, "Come again?"

Polland, "We're fucked, someone grassed everyone".

Becksy breathed out and went, "Really, really".

Polland sat down and said, "And there is nothing to be done about it".

Becksy shrugged and said, "You sure we can't just grease the wheels of a judge, you know pay them off?"

Poland shook his head, "Nah man, this is the uncorruptible Judge down in Manchester, they call him judge fudge."

Becksy shrugged and said, "Why do they call him Judge Fudge?"

Polland sighed and replied, "Because he hands out prison sentences like sweets".

Becksy produced a packet of fags and crashed one to Polland. "Oh," he said as he clicked his zippo shut after lighting Polland's fag. "You know Gramps is gonna throw a fit when he hears this."

Polland smoked on and said, "I leave that up to you mate".

Becksy saw Polland out after a couple of beers and half a packet of fags. Polland walked away and headed back into Edinburgh city centre to catch his train down to Manchester. Becksy went back to his bed and took another couple of jellies. Seen as he had ruined the last two with beer. He fell into an unusual sleep, one haunted by premonition and omens. The devils again had the YBC by the balls. And all the angels in heaven wouldn't come to their rescue. Yes, things were getting strange and it was a sweat filled cold turkey kind of sleep. He knew that, that news was about as welcome as a case of herpes in a nunnery. They had to be careful. Maybe even close down certain connections and move gracefully and hope that they didn't get caught red handed.

CHAPTER 10

Grandad finished having sex with Tequila and they both made plans to meet in a day or so. Gramps walked home and into his house. His mam welcomed him into the house. "Your pal Scott was on the phone. He said you need to meet him urgently".

Grandad put the kettle on and said, "Scott, Scott Shaw?"

Lorna carried on with her puzzle book, "Aye Scott Shaw, the boy fae Broomie"'.

Grandad smiled and made a brew. "Aye I'll phone him as soon as I've had this cuppa," he carried on making the brew. "

Oh, and an envelope from the DSS arrived".

Grandad smiled and said as his mother handed him the brown envelope, "It's just my fortnightly Giro" and he opened the envelope. It was as he said a giro for two hundred and seventy-five pounds. He looked at the Giro and said to his mum "You need Digs?"

She blew out her smoke, smiled and replied, "aye son".

Grandad produced his roll of twenties, "How much you needing Mam?"

She carried on smiling and said, "About three hundred for the month".

He smiled and counted out the three hundred pounds and gave it to her.

"Thank you, Laddie". She went back to her puzzle book.

Grandad phoned Becksy and waited for an answer.

"We got problems," came the statement from Becksy,

Grandad listened intently to his compadre'.

"Wo, Wo, settle Petal when was Polland up and why didn't he come directly tae me?"

Becksy just snorted a short breath, "He didn't want anything to come along too soon".

Grandad paused for second, "Was he paranoid and stoned?" asked Gramps.

Becksy laughed, "No, no really".

"I mean some people take to pressure and enjoy the thrill. Does that sound like your amigo?"

Grandad continued, "Polland is super fucking cool". Gramps and him had went taxing punters and taking pieces of dope from them. Sometimes they went robbing bikes. But that was back in the day. And he had found Polland to be, well, somebody you could trust and also someone who watched your back. They had dated around the same gang of lassies. Simone, Claire, Fiona and some others who didn't last long in their company. Anyway, Grandad was worried about this.

"He said we've got four weeks before they come down on us and I mean come down on us, us all Grandad".

Leon glared off into the distance. He hadn't a clue into what to do. "We need to have a sit down with the Other chiefs" Gramps smiled things were changing, an old oriental saying 'embrace change as if it was your friend and it will help.' He knew in his heart that he had trouble on the horizon. Maybe even a little time. That was if they caught them red handed. But however, the consequences would only strengthen their resources. He would send out the word that it was only a minor problem and Grandad would do the right thing and that was to make sure that business flowed as best they could.

The other Chiefs in the YBC were putting out the feelers trying to ascertain whether they needed to close down certain drug runs. The Manchester one mainly. It would be the main one that was pipping in and bringing the most profit. Grandad had a sudden brainstorm, send the drugs further south and sit on it until the Bizzies had finished their search and seizure. It would cause a minor drought, but they had time to think on what to do. And when everything was calm and the coast was clear they could begin to gradually feed the dealers. And they would keep business strictly to the regulars. They would start slowly to build up the product sales because he and his family were known to be major sellers of drugs. He had his big toe stuck in that shit. But the lord willing he would be one step ahead of the DS. I mean someone was getting paid to turn in his amigos. And Grandad searched out Kingo and his brother as they were the slippiest dealers around.

Grandad spoke with a couple of the Chiefs and said that they were going to have to meet up so as Gramps could lay down the plans of re-diverting the product. This meant they would go into a drought and they would have to listen intently to the scanners and Kingo who had his connection in the Polis knew exactly what to listen for. Gramps and him had a meeting. Where Grandad laid down the whole plan to make them seem as if they were unable to keep business flowing. But this was a false sense of security. And would hopefully keep the Polis from shutting them down totally. It was a stroke of genius and Grandad had very little faith, but he knew that Kingo would come up aces. He was a genius. He was still wanted for the Gauntlet raid. But Kingo smiled knowing that he was one step ahead of the Bizzies and loved the whole thing, you know breaking the law.

His brother James had been out for ages and they had caused so much damage that the police were dumbfounded. And the Sheriff was not able to keep up with the damage they were doing. But that was only part of the whole scheme. Polland had finally got hold of the Sergeant that was being paid to keep stum, He was all apologizes but reminded Polland that nothing was set in stone and that things change. Polland reminded him that he had a nice house and a decent way of life, but this could all change. The Sergeant smiled sorrowfully and said, "Do what you got to do".

Polland snarled down the receiver, "You just don't get it, you fuck. We own you, you are only breathing good free air 'cause we pay you. And the closer they get to the Chiefs closer you get to be a riding toy in Strangeways Prison." The Sergeant sighed and said, "No choice huh?"

Polland snarled and replied, "No choice". Polland then hung up and walked away. All the Chiefs were going to gather in two days and that was just 'cause it was an emergency. They had to drop everything and figure a way out of the shitty situation, They had all been grassed and as the Lou Reed song said, "You're gonna reap just what you sow".

Biscuit was on the blower calming his regulars down. This went on for a day and a night. And Biscuit was exhausted at the end of it. Suzzane kept him rolled and toked. He needed the dope just to keep his nerves steady. And the panic, well it was something they had foreseen. And Grandad had a way of producing miracles, Ways within ways. He was definitely a genius in the game. He stopped shipments from up north. And only ran a little of the smack and nothing else. But that was a major bug bear with the Polis. They knew that it would be there for the taking, but somehow the stuff disappeared before they got near it. Like a said they knew how to sell the stuff without putting themselves at risk of being busted, and the smack, well they were doubly careful. Making drops at roadside cafes and knowing where the police were positioned and where was the best and most advantaged places to meet. And they changed Mules. One month by bus another by train and yet another by Hells Angels, and you know the police are shit feared o them.

They tended to travel in packs and they were armed. Grandad smiled as the streets were in a code of silence only Gramps and Biscuit knew how many rings on the phone and where the stuff was headed. The meet came around and Grandad smiled and said to himself as the house began to fill with the Chiefs. They all sat down and began to discuss how their patch was doing and when should they ease up and let the product flow free again. Grandad who had the foresight to know when and where the stuff was safest began to outlay a plan keeping their connections safe and control the punters. Lay-ons and tick were strictly to regulars and they were not to mount up as they were extremely vulnerable.

Grandad finished by saying, "We're lucky my Mucker fae Manchester got news of their impending action. He was quick to act and he didn't use the blower, which is the wisest of moves, He hopped straight on a train came all the way up here and got hold of Becksy".

Biscuit smiled, "Yeah we are fortunate to have advance warning on the Police and there impending action," he said.

Grandad smiled and they all got slowly stoned. The finalised the plan of action then sent out the word, "to be careful." Again, they narrowly missed being caught with their pants down. The meet finished and Gramps was filled with drugs just for having the foresight of the busts.

Biscuit smiled and nodded at Grandad, who knew that it was bang on. And his reward was an ounce of cocaine. Pure, white and smooth. He also got handed a bag full of Acid tabs, thirty strawberries double dipped. He smiled and put the two bags into his pocket. He then headed to Pinkies den. Biscuit offered him a lift but Grandad replied, "Nah man we're clear for the next day or so".

Pinkie smiled rolled over and lit a fag, he hadn't heard the news yet, but Grandad was about tae spring it on him. He opened the door and walked into the living room.

Pinkie shouted through to Grandad. "Awright mate?"

Grandad smiled sat down and began to rack up two lines for each of them. Pinkie came through saw what he was a doing and said, "someone got paid".

Gramps smiled and carried on never taking his eyes of the prize and said, "Someone got lucky".

Pinkie took his two lines.

"You know we're being forced into a drought," said Grandad.

Pinkie Squeaked his teeth, smiled a cocaine smile and replied, "No, why, what's happening?"

Grandad told Pinkie what was happening. He didn't look too shocked. But then Pinkie was immune to bad news. He had this way of dealing with harsh situations. Then when it came time for action he would fly straight like an arrow, straight and to the point. And he never missed his mark. He was clever and savage at the same time. I know, I know, you would think that the two didn't mix but Pinkie had made stress an art form and was ready at any moment, I mean he had proved his worth with diligence when he was in the Tin Pail and whilst they were at war with the Skulls. This was different though. Someone was grassing and I mean healthy grassing. Nobody was safe and the clock was ticking away to the time that they were all going to be busted.

Grandad was the man with the plan and that was why he had just been paid. They sat and rocked and racked a good quarter of coke and were having a ball. Pinkie smiled as the conversation came round to what were they going to do. Gramps smiled and lit up his bubble.

Pinkie asked, "You heard fae Giz?"

Grandad smiled and smoke left his lungs. "Nah man he's loved up. Nothing can touch him you know that".

Pinkie laughed "He's one lucky, lucky laddie".

Gramps nodded his head and said, "I know this, you know this, but do you think that Giz knows this?"

Pinkie smiled and picked up the bubble loaded it and toked. "Probably not," he said as he breathed out the vapour.

"Anyway we just have to be diligent the next couple of months, and no going to war".

Pinkie laughed at the statement and replied, "Why do I get the feeling I'm the one who is getting told that"

Gramps smiled and replied, "Aye well your hardly mister diplomatic, when it comes to a scrap".

Pinkie nodded and laughed, "and you are?"

Grandad let out a chuckle. "Nah man I don't think either of us are".

Pinkie carried on laughing. This session went on for most of the day into the night. Lamby was in Grandad's mind. And he thought that he had went away. Nobody went near him, nobody relied on him, he was poison. Anyway, he had done a vanishing act after Paki had been dealt wae. I mean the loose ends were well taken care of. Grandad sat back and said no, this rat knew everything and had taken a painstaking time to enforce his treachery. That's why Polland had shown up on Becksy's door. Knowing he may have been shadowed. I mean the polis had their fingers everywhere they were just turning into a fist. One that was going to cripple the Y.B.C.

Grandad looked Pinkie in the eye, he was of the same faith as Grandad and that was, he wasn't scared of doing time, but knew it would be hard time with the lifers. Grandad was if the opinion, 'Dinea dae the crime if you canea dae the time'. He lived by this; he revelled in this. It gave him courage. Knowing that he wasn't the only one who was up against it. No, he smiled and carried on trying to figure out who was selling them out. Then it occurred to him that it could be a few of them a network of grasses. Grandad drifted into a sleep, a few of them was whirring through his mind. Certain faces were popping up as possibilities. Jimmy Boyle a lad down in Manchester, Beefy, Nah no the Beefster, Lamby. He was definite candidate, as he had tried to set Grandad up with a hit. Grandad slept on.

CHAPTER 11

Paul woke that night early morning. He reached over for the spliff that he had ready to kick his day. But something was up, something just wasn't quite right. He knew the Polis were onto him and the Northern connection. This was already known to everyone. His punters were going elsewhere. The stash he was holding onto was getting moved, nothing was left to chance. And I mean nothing, Grandad was staying a step ahead of the DS. How they had managed to collect the information was sheer luck and Grandad was going to stamp down on the situation and they were going to come up wae nothing.

They were cold, cold plans and it would show when the Dens all stopped dealing and the Polis had nothing and just as he thought about it everywhere went silent, as the riot police surrounded several dens where allegedly the bulk of the narcotics was being shifted to, then cooked and passed on. They stood, riot shields ready in Mosside Manchester and in several other areas in Manchester. The Battering Rams were brought forth to the doors of each Den. Then the whistle went and they counted to five and entered the flats leaving nothing to chance. And silence, no hassle, no ruckus. No, they had been sold out. Their grasses had sold them on to a bum steer, a Harvey Rabbit, something that wasn't there.

Grandad smiled an evil smile into the night air as he sat and drained a jug of Lager. Pinkie smiled and laughed and said, "Now can I have a bigger slice?"

Grandad settled down and said, "Yes mate you can have extra but it's for you and its personal, nobody must know".

Pinkie smiled and got him and Gramps another jug of beer. The whole of Broomie was dry as a stick. And they all wore the same smile, "Goin Grandad" was what everybody was saying. They never missed a beat and the street it belonged to the street. Grandad smiled some more as Cha and Raymie entered Misfits. Grandad stood up and Cha gripped wrists wae him. Raymie was next to make wrists wae him. They sat and got a good drunk on, the four of them. Giz arrived near the end of the night wae Janice. She too was told tae pull her socks up and had done so, she too believed in Grandad as he was proving more and more invaluable and she trusted her sister's taste in men. Never brought the wrong man tae her door yet. And that was plain tae see as she was quite happy with her choice in men. Grandad being the crowning achievement. He had come up and come up fast. Growing wider and wider and filling with knowledge and street power.

The music in the pub was *Five to One* the Doors classic. And it was followed by an assortment of songs By Meatloaf, Queen, Doctor Hook and Pulp. But the Polis being duped didn't let it slide they were lining up another attempt at stopping the Angel Hair smack. Again, Grandad got a call and again they emptied and moved elsewhere. What you had going was a big game of Cops and Robbers. Still, nobody was busted, still the product was safe and stashed, waiting for the all clear. And Grandad smiled as he became richer and richer. And more respected. He kept a tight leash on the Narcotics and time after time he was one step ahead of the DS.

Then like magic the police eased off them. Gramps was still ahead and staying that way. There was a gun amnesty and a knife amnesty. Then they began to ease up on the cannabis situation. Decriminalized it was a sure thing, I mean America had done so in two or three different states, and Amsterdam was, well it was, a groom's choice for a stag night. They had peace and it was contented it was safe, and it kept everyone happy. Grandad was watching the stash cashes and money cashes grow. Pinkie was satisfied with another ten per cent of the money landing in his pocket. Gramps gripped onto himself, as power like that, well it was overpowering. Really it was messing with his noodle. He decided to take Tequila on a cruise around Brazil. He decided to stay straight the whole four-week cruise as did Tequila. I mean they drank, Rum mostly and rum cocktails. They were completely at ease. If anyone asked, they were owners of a construction company. It didn't matter that he was one of the most sought-after criminals in Britain. He had spun the dime took his time made his mark and enforced it. Grandad was legendary. Him and the Y.B.C.

CHAPTER 12

Grandad got back after three months of sailing around Brazil. And Grandad got the chance to go and pay his respects to the Gracies. They were certainly popular, and it was like ine if them things that holy men do a pilgrimage. He was happy to be in the same city as the Gracies. The Dojo was pristine with proper equipment and you could smell the adrenaline and sweat. They were just finishing off a class and Grandad bowed and entered.

"I'm just taking a look around".

The sensei smiled and asked, "what discipline are you?"

Grandad didn't need an invite to announce his style of Karate do. "The way of the fist shozu kai".

The Sensai carried on asking questions and Grandad was honoured to be there. "What belt are you?"

Grandad smiled and said "Green".

The Sensai smiled and walked away and came back with a T-shirt saying, "A gift, you watch much MMA?"

Grandad smiled and said, "Every chance I get".

The Sensei put out his hand then said. "It was nice to meet a fellow martial artist from Scotland, Edinburgh you had said?"

Grandad shook his hand with a medium grip, knowing that to be over enthusiastic would be out and being humble was best. He took the T-shirt smiled at Tequlia and they headed back to the cruise ship. It dawned on him later that the guy was only Conan Silveria famed for having twenty-eight fights fought and only one loss. Grandad smiled folded up the T-shirt and said, "I'm going back to the Karate, soon as we get back from this cruise and I'm gonna rub Chrissy Begs nose in it".

Well, the cruise became more boozy as they headed back to port and they were brown as brown sugar, Tequilas skin took a freckled glow to it and the two of them had had a wonderful time. They got back and everyone was jealous. But credit where credit was due. They had saved over four million pounds worth of gear. And the police were left scratching their heads.

⚜

What happened asked the MP, who had the stats of the busts in front of him?

"He got wind if us that's all." said the Chief of Police to the Home Office leader, which was not wise, he then spent the next hour giving the Chief it tight. Take truncheon out and insert into own arse.

"We spent years and years of man hours went into that search and seizure, it shouldn't have missed a beat" The PM was not amused and again balled him out. "You get whoever done this, who organized this and plug our leak?"

The Chief smiled a half entry smile. Then left "Not even a cup of tea…" he murmured as he went back to New Scotland Yard. He looked at the board where all the players in this, so sudden, tragic farce were pinned up. One of them in particular was circled with a red marker pen, 'Leon James Gratton. Aka Grandad.

He called in his secretary, "Can I have a cup of tea Delores".

She came through and put the teacup down with a biscuit on the side. He started to go through the transcripts of various dealers who had been captured but with only a small amount of powder or a few tablets of ecstasy. LSD was popping up everywhere and the rave season was almost over. They had just drawn the short straw and were eager pawns in a game of street chess and Grandad was taking his time. He was enjoying romantic time with Sheila and it was hot and heavy. They brought the luggage in and started to settle down. Tequila rolled a joint. And Grandad smiled and produced some powder fae his stash. Racked up a couple of lines two for him and two for Tequila.

They took them and began to relax. With the time they spent they were knackered. They needed a holiday from the holiday. They went to bed and listened to Absolute Nineties the song was *I'm Not buying I'm just Looking* by Stereophonics. Things I want things I think I want. They dozed off in each other's embrace. Things were normal for the next week or so, they made the most out of the end of summer. Then as they grew weary someone changed the rules again.

No, Grandad was not expecting this to happen. He was sitting in his mam's house enjoying a good pin of angel when all he heard was the door being rammed. He gritted his teeth as the Police (Armed) swarmed over him. He was on his knees in two seconds flat. The growling of the police was so loud that Grandad was practically deaf. And for the next two or three hours all he could hear was ringing. They took him tae Saint Leonards Police Station, where he had to wait a good two to three hours until the ringing in his ears stopped then the Bizzies decided to interrogate him.

Grandad had fuck all tae say. Still, they grilled him and grilled him hard. They tried the soft approach, giving him a fag and a cup of tea. Grandad smoked the fag but didn't touch the tea, they asked, "Why don't you drink the tea?"

Grandad snarled down his left side and said, "I only drink my mams tea".

He was cold and sophisticated. Not a quivering wreck like most gangsters were when faced with the armed Police. Grandad was stony-faced and knew he had nothing to lose, It was the weekend and court wasn't back until the Monday afternoon, That was when the summons took place and the prisoners were housed down in the Sherrif's Dungeons and boy did it smell like a Dungeon. Acrid and you could taste the unwashed prisoners who had no change of clothes or razors or deodorant. Nah it smelled like shit. And the concussion was beginning to wear off by the second day.

The polis smiled and turned off the recorder and said, "We got you by the Goolies San. Play ball we might reduce your sentence?"

Grandad again stony-faced, perfectly turned and replied, "No comment".

They laughed and said, "The hiding you're going to take when you hit Gen Pop".

Grandad maintained his non-committal stance, "Nae comment".

Soon as he got into the dock the Sherrif just responded, "Eighteen months, no Parole" Grandad smiled, looked at the sheriff and said, "Cheers mate I could use a break".

The Sherriff looked at him and nodded, "Take him away".

He was suited and booted. Saughton B wing was where he was headed. He arrived and was immediately surrounded by the whistles and jeers and some even clapped him. Talk about striking a blow for the Gangland mentality. He had made them proud. And at the same time made himself very rich. He got his head down and carried on the with the feeling that it was going to be a quick eighteen months. If he behaved himself he would get some of his term reduced. No fighting, no aggravating the screws. No dealing, no running his mouth, which was basically aggravating the screws. He walked into his single cell and on the bunk was a tranny and some backie. He sat down rolled a roll up and had a puff, the door was open, and he could hear how much appreciation the other convicts had for him. He smiled and, on the radio, came the House of Pain song *Hard Rock Hero of the Neighbourhood*. The radio DJ then sent a shout out tae all the convicts in B hall.

Grandad was just at home as he was at home. Grandad smiled and listened all day to the Tranny. Inside the baccy was a few pound coins enough to get him some vallies. Or some Juice. He decided on the vallies and had them just before he went tae sleep. He had a great night's sleep. He woke the next day and got a shower. He smiled as he brushed his hair and went down for breakfast. He had tea and toast not the greatest cup o' tea. But that didn't matter he knew that he had to keep his nails clean. And there was no animosity between him and the rest of the Cons. In fact, they knew him and knew what he had done. He was the only one brave enough to face off in the deadly game of chess that was the Streets.

A couple of the meat heads looked at him and walked over. "You'll be Grandad?"

"Aye," he replied.

"My name is Beano". The other guy looked around and Grandad thought if these guys were any bigger they would have blocked out the sun.

The other guy smiled and said, "I'm Skull".

Grandad let out a little chuckle and said, "Corse you are".

They both smiled and said, "Anything you need if we can't get it you we'll pay you".

Gramps smiled and sat eating his cereal. "Thanks guys".

The two tanks rolled away smiling. Grandad thought 'what a pleasant surprise' Then headed back tae his cell. He began to roll a couple of rollies and sat back and had a nap. The radio was giving him spirit and he knew nothing would pop off. He felt like a celebrity and the one thing that was immense tae him was the fact that they had shifted all their gear and the angel hair pipeline had started again. They were top of the table again. They re-evaluated the product and how much they needed straight away and how much they would need to stash to keep the bloodhounds fae their door.

Grandad put in the call to make sure everything was okay. "Cha my main man?"

Cha smiled and took a couple of tokes from the joint he had. "Sad news, they got you bang tae rights."

Gramps smiled as he could smell the weed being smoked round about him.

"Cha will you pop doon tae Manchester and sort something oot fur aes?"

Cha smiled. "Aye nae bother Grandad. Is it an action or a piece o' work?"

Grandad smiled and replied, "I need you take flex some muscle".

Cha smiled and roached his joint. "Aye as long as a get the poppy fur it, me and Raymie will hop right tae it". Cha smiled and thought it aint cheap but digging the knife in was something that Cha and Raymie were known to dae. They had completed a number of actions. And they had done it expertly. No mistake no noise just a blade tae the back or guts depending what kind of message they were to send. If it was a personal request they did the guts. If it was a message they did the back. Grandad looked around and thought I better phone Tequila.

She was in the middle of cooking some Pot, this was done every now and then and it was the best way to take a bong. They rubbed the cannabis and tobacco together on the stove and packed their bong and yeah well you know the rest.

"Where have you been?" she said down the phone.

Grandad said, "I've been huckled."

Tequila smiled. "What jail?"

Grandad relaxed "Saughton B wing gen pop".

"Okay well it could be worse," she replied.

Grandad lit one of his rollies and took a good drag. "Can you make sure the Northern lights is still getting shipped to Manchester?"

She almost fell about laughing. "I got my ane connections you ken that."

Grandad said the magic word. "Please go on please".

She smiled and the bong bubbled as she took a lung full. "Aye why not, I'll get Janice tae help me". She smiled then went back tae her Bong. This was a bit of a hassle, but she knew that she could handle it. And Janice well she was natural businesswoman and could hold her own if anything popped off. Tequila was having a bit of a party with the girls; Janice wasn't there as she was loved up wae Gizmo.

⚜

Gizmo woke at about three thirty in the am. And went straight for a beer and a piss. He stopped at the table and looked at the pile of white on the table. He bobbed over it and took two lines. Janice was lying snoring a small feminine snore. He smiled then got back into bed.

He remembered when he and Janice had first got together and that made him smile all the more. He was really hooked on her. It was out of place for him, but he knew there was no other way to be than loved up. And it wasn't just the drugs. No something like this did'nea come along every day. He smiled and let the cool, cool rush of cocaine. Make his night that little more lush.

⚜

Pinkie smiled as he ended up at Becksy's door. He gave a good knock on the wooden door and waited. Becksy smiled and said, "You okay Pinkie?"

Pinkie smiled and said, "Aye man I'm sound. You need any white or maybe a tab?"

Becksy smiled and said, "Nah man I'm sound".

Pinkie produced a ready rolled joint.

"That's twice Grandad has made a name for Broomie," said Becksy.

Pinkie handed the joint tae Becksy.

Becksy said, "Gracias" and took his time knowing that tonight was gonna be wild. "How is Gramps anyway?"

Pinkie smiled and said, "Saughton B wing".

Becksy just about collapsed a lung with the coughing he had. "Why am I no surprised" he said.

Pinkie smiled and dropped a strawberry. "You wana go tripping with me?"

Becksy smiled and said, "nah man I'm going up toon tae tipplers wae Nessy, CC and Beefy".

Pinkie was too late the buzz had started and it was only a few hours before he peaked. "I'll catch up wae yie the morrow," said Pinkie then he rambled on. He put in the earphones and began tae listen tae some tunes being as it was his favourite Depeche Mode *Exciter*.

'Can you feel a little love' Came pumping through his MP3 player. This was going to be one hell of a night. He walked up the road to the area off of Spylaw. He was tripping out his face and the Strawberry gleamed and gave of the right kind of buzz and the music well it was perfect. And Pinkie had several of their albums on his MP3 player. He was sound, nothing could touch him. He had taken his ten per cent in product knowing that the viper pay was great when it panned out. He was settling into a pure biorhythmic kick that you only got fae a decent tab of acid. He carried on walking whilst the pavement crawled and the buildings bounced and the rush well the rush was proper cool. He burped and it was like the most tummy rushing feeling ever. Oh, he was cool. It was just going dark at nine thirty and Pinkie couldnea be any more in good shape. And that was down tae the buzz of a strawberry that was going to take up most o' the night. He smiled hunkered down and thought, 'I can carry on crawling or I can carry on rushing.' It was theses decisive times, in which he knew where he stood.

The scene from Hellraiser came into his head, "What's you pleasure sir?" He smiled but let the horror go. He carried on stopping to go to McDonalds for a burger. Then back into the neon wilderness. He was really having a ball. He finished the burger and walked out tae his den. He smiled and sneezed a small sneeze but even that was amazing. It tickled and sent him popping along, he had about three hours left and then he would be coming down. He sat down and put on *The Thief and the Cobbler*, with its Arabian colours and tripped out patterns. He was engrossed, the smiling acid checks the weird colourful patterns, no, this was better than any fucking Disney. He smiled as the evil ruler's eyes twirled and he was oot his face.

Becksy, Beefy, CC and Nessy couldn't help but want to see the state Pinkie was in so after they finished drinking, they went and peeped at him through the window. He was tripping oot his nut. He was glued tae the telly and his eyes were shining all kinds of highs. He was totally gone. The film finished so he put on Tron. Again, glued tae the telly every now and then, he'd whoop and holler at the telly. Beefy and the rest of them watched as he tripped on.

"Hey Pinkie," said Beefy in a loud booming voice. "This is God, I have a mission for you".

Pinkie listened intently, "I want you to take your stash and leave it on CC's stair well". Pinkie went and got his stash and put his jacket on then headed along to CC's hoose. He put the stash next to his front door. Then headed home to his den. He sat down switched the film back on and carried on peeking. Then Beefy who was really enjoying it smiled and again boomed forth, "Pinkie." He boomed and Pinkie was hook lined and sinkered.

"Yes, almighty one", Beefy nearly blew the gag but stained calm. "You have some Beer in your house?"

Pinkie smiled nervously "Yes Lord".

"Put it outside the library."

Pinkie gathered all the beer, seven eight bottles and left them on the ground next to the library. He then came back inside, Becksy grabbed them and took them to the other three. The four of them popped their bottles and began to finish of Pinkies stash o' cargo. Beefy let oot a very, very large belch and said, "Bless you my son".

Pinkie smiled and began tae come doon. Pinkie carried on and Beefy and the rest of them went home. Soon as they got a safe distance away, they began tae laugh. Pinkie fell into a sleep and was none the wiser. He didn't even leave himself a bottle of beer.

CHAPTER 13

Grandad lit the rollie and sat down and listened tae his tranny. He was listening to Classic Rock. And was well, in better shape than what he thought he would be. The Screws were coming and going wae him and he was being watched after by two of the biggest convicts you had ever seen. Beano and Skull. He was called Beano 'cause he had choked someone to death with a Beano comic. Skull on the other hand, well you don't want to know. Gruesome. To put it plainly. Nah it was better to stay on good terms with them. He thought that anyone who had a beef with those two was obviously insane. As they were never getting out and well, they were massive. Obviously, they ran B hall. The rest of jail was well, well under the Governor's control. But some whispers that he was queer hawking bendo. and lilly chickened roaming dandie.

Grandad hadn't met the Governor. He was too busy he was doing paperwork and arranging day release for the model prisoners. It was just a rumour, but it was one the hardened convicts who kept tae themselves. He was due tae see his brief next week whilst he continued to lobby the penal system that it was a case of misguided justice and well, well they had the wrong man. He was hoping that he would have a satisfactory result within the next four to six weeks. It was still ongoing. And Grandad, well they didn't treat royalty the way the treated Grandad. The tranny blasted out Thin Lizzy *Whiskey in the Jar*. Just as the song finished Skull was at his cell door wae a small bottle of rum. Grandad smiled and took the bottle and then. Beano arrived at his cell door and gave him six tins of Relentless. He smiled and mixed the two in a plastic cup. It was like rocket fuel and sent him careering into a drunken state. He smiled and stayed up most of the night listening tae his tranny and drinking the rocket fuel.

He finished the bottle and smiled. "Well, that'll be that". He then began tae smile and fell into a three-hour coma, which was rudely interrupted by breakfast. Again, the golden treatment. He had saved a lot of these inmates from more time. As the bizzies had got the connections right but no product, Grandad smiled again. He was a genius con man. And had no hangover. He drank the last tin of relentless and went and got tea and cereal. The governor was swamped with people handing themselves in. Just to get next tae the crime prince.

He was approached by Beano again who smiled. "The prison Tattooist is offering some free work," he said tae Grandad.

Gramps smiled and said, "I've always wanted a joker tattoo".

Beano smiled and walked away. He came by about an hour and a half later. "Aye man. The tattooist Ronnie will come along wae various sketches. And you can take your pick".

Grandad smiled and said, "Cheers man". Beano walked away and headed back tae his cell.

Grandad rubbed his hands together and said, "You know when you've done a good turn".

Later that day the Tattooist came round. "Okay me old China, take a look at these?" He then brought out several sketches of Jokers both comic book and traditional. Grandad looked at each of them smiled and said pointing at the most sinister one a joker with a smoking gun.

"That's smart," Ronnie smiled and said, "Where dae yie want it?"

Grandad smiled "The forearm wrist side I think".

Ronnie produced his tattoo gun and broke out a fresh needle. Then he started to shave the area and mop it down with disinfectant. Then he began to sketch the picture on his arm. Then came the buzz, and slight numbing. Grandad was a virgin tae the tattoo game heard fae various pals, "aye the hurt like hell but hey they are worth the pain". Nichol had said this take him.

Grandad sat the good part of two hours as the guy who was smiling as he got on with the job he asked the question. "How did you suss the police so fast?"

Grandad smiled winced a little then said, "Skill and knowing where to position my drugs".

Ronnie laughed "Simple as that" Grandad nodded his head and replied, "Simple as that" Ronnie shook his head smiled and carried on, "so word came down and you were struck by a lightning idea".

Gramps nodded as the guy wiped away some blood, "Well man there are a lot of people in here, thanking you".

Grandad smirked "Yeah I suppose there would be," replied Grandad.

He carried on with the Tattoo and smiled as the realisation that he was Putting Ink on a Legend.

"Well, it was worth it," said Grandad. The tattoo was finished and Grandad was happy with the Joker on his arm, the skinny crime prince of Jokers was holding a revolver that was smoking as if just fired. Grandad's eyes glazed over as he looked at the piece of art on the underside of his arm. He was proud and he never really felt it. He got on with the rest of the day. Before Ronnie left he asked, "You need dope. H or some Charlie just tell either Beano or Skull and they will sort you out street prices for you".

Grandad smiled. "Aye nae bother". Then he rolled a roll up and sat down. Grandad said to himself, "I hope tae get oot soon as". Then lay on his bunk.

⚜

Pinkie woke and went tae the fridge to get a beer. "Nope nane". He said then he went to get his stash. "Gone fuck". He had no idea something about God. "God came and claimed my stash and my beer". He then began to piece the whole night together. "Yep, fucking God". Pinkie's eyes began to water and he screamed, "Fucking God took my Beer and my stash!"

The first thing he was going tae do was contact a priest and see if he could make head nor tail of it. It was a mystery, a complete scratch your head mystery. He was going tae church and the Priest better have an answer. He walked to the church on the edge of Wester Hailes.

He smiled, took the song book then went and spoke tae the Priest. "I've had an awakening sir".

The small middle-aged man with the white collar smiled, "yes my son tell me all about it?"

Pinkie started to recount what he could remember about the voice of God.

The Preacher stood and listened. "You are telling me you were on mind altering substances, and God got you to put your stash of drugs onto someone's doorstep, then he got you to leave all your beer at the door of the library. Then after five minutes or so he belched and thanked you".

"Yes" came the reply fae Pinkie.

The Preacher who hadn't heard a joke in what must have been a lifetime, smiled and said, "Well one you are a Lunatic".

Pinkie looked at the man with his mouth open, "Two you are a Junky".

Pinkie waited for the rest, "You were tricked probably by your friends".

But Pinkie was still positive it was really God. He went to complain, but the Priest had already walked away laughing.

All Pinkie could say was "Oh!" He then headed round tae his mum's house. Giz was talking and laughing with someone on the Phone. It was Becksy. Pinkie smiled and sat down on the doorstep and lit a fag.

Giz came and sat next tae him. "I hear you been talking tae God".

Pinkie laughed and said, "It was Beefy, he wae the rest a them eh?"

Pinkie smiled, "so where did I take my stash?"

Giz laughed, "you left it at CC's door, daftie".

"Becksy has got it, he says your lucky that Beefy didnea tan it".

Pinkie smiled, "I just contacted the clergy an everything, claiming it was a sign fae God". He then spammed himself and spoke. "I'm a fucking doughnut."

Pinkie smiled and began tae laugh at the whole thing.

CHAPTER 14

Tequila walked down the road after getting the news about Grandad. She was walking tae see if his Brief had any word on a release date. She got round to Mcrann's Criminal Justice. She entered and walked up to the petit blonde at reception.

"It's Sheila, right?" she said. then buzzed through tae Mcrann. "It's Ms Thompson at my desk sir".

He smiled and said, "send her though Gail".

Sheila walked through and began to sit down,

She stopped and Mcrann pointed to the seat "please" he said as she sat. "Well Ms Thompson, my whole office is dedicated to the release of your partner, we are running various of ideas at the Sherrif and the PF. I'm lobbying all the time in the hope of getting his sentence, not just decreased, but clear and him set free".

She smiled and rested her eyes for a second. "I want tae ken who signed his warrant, and I want a full exoneration and I want him compensated for the time he did under duress".

Mcrann smiled, "Yes Sheila," and he stretched forth his hand to hers and shook it.

She smiled, knowing that he was having a fling wae his secretary. 'I mean you'd hau to be gay tae no want to saddle that. Sheila was nae Bi-sexual and she had tae admit even she would have a wild romp wae her'. She smiled and headed back up the road. She would pop into Grandad's mam's and tell her how she got on. She did so and sat and had a chin wag wae her then off she went back tae her house.

⚜

Grandad looked up from the junk induced gouch he was having. The door opened and Gramps knew this wasn't standard time by a screw, no he was getting paid a visit. One of the screws was well juiced up about what had happened down south and knew there was a small bomb on his head just tae leave a couple of marks, you know a broken rib and a black eye, he hadn't seen it coming and hadn't long shot his small bag of kit. He was lucky that he had stashed the works and it was a screw and his pet. This was a nightmare as he was too wasted to put up a fight and fine they knew it. The pet held him whilst the screw bludgeoned him with his baton. Then after he was sure he had done enough damage he stopped. Grandad just scowled and never made a sound. He fell on to his bunk and tried to keep his head clear.

"See you next week," said, the screw.

Grandad decided to wait until morning then tell the screw on watch he fell. The screw opened the door and could hear Gramps wheezing with the knocks he had taken.

"Who's the fucking animal son?"

Grandad spat some blood in the toilet and said, "I fell Boss".

"Not bleeding likely." Then he called for the other screws to take him to the infirmary. Everybody was keeping shtum. They all got on with their rituals, tea, cereal and shaving. Grandad was laid up for a total of four days and four nights. He was given honour visits during which his mam and Tequila visited him. They brought baccy and juice. The dogs got a sniff but nothing amiss. He smiled as they appeared for a second day in which Tequila noticed the tattoo. "When did you get that?

"Three or four days ago," he said and she sat and looked at him.

"That'll be your virginity broken," she smiled she had to admit it was a touch of class. One of those things that pop and well shock. But it was smart, yes it was, done just right. And it suited him down tae a tee. He smiled and they got onto the subject about Pinkie and the Force of God. He tried to stop laughing as his ribs were fucked and hurt like hell to even move, but laugh, yeah it wasn't easy, but he did after the story finished.

"So, we have a believer in our crew". He then winced with pain. "Next they'll be locking him up in the Looney bin".

She smiled and said, "I hope no they guys are mental".

Grandad laughed again and winced with pain again. "Ohhh, its fucking sare leave me in peace woman".

Grandad got his pillows fluffed as the nurse said, "That your woman, she's braw she always keeps you on your toes?"

Grandad smiled, breathed in then took a couple of pain relief tablets. Morphine. He smiled and fell into the chemical wasteland of sleep that only came with poppy. And you know what I mean by Poppy. He finished his stint in the infirmary and was sent back to his cell. Grandad counted the days three more and I bet they try to make me a whore. Beano and Skull arrived after lunch and Beano smiled, "Awright Grandad heard what happened".

Grandad smiled and as Beano said this, "aye well I'll be seeing him when I get oot".

Skull laughed, "everybody ken he was at it. But no one wants to disagree wie him they found one o' his pets friends hanging in the shower room".

Grandad spoke "Bent?"

Beano laughed then said, "Then some".

"I bet you two don't get messed wae," said Grandad.

Beano who pointed at a scar on his neck. "Twelve of them and that was all they got after I finished wae them," He smiled. "They were mopping up their shit and blood for a week". He laughed a little un-nerving laugh.

Grandad smiled and looked at the pair of them. "They tell you when they will be back?"

Gramps snarled "Aye at the end of this week" Skull laughed "I can give you a chib?" Grandad smiled, "I think that would only make things worse".

"Aye well I'll check on you every day, if I dinea then Skull will".

Grandad thanked the two heavy-built convicts then went back tae his reading. He smiled as he carried on reading *'The Puppet Masters'* by Robert Heinlen. He fell into a Valium and painkiller sleep. He had a hard couple of days to face, he only hoped that Sheila would come through on the law side of things, he would see her in the middle of next week. Hopefully he would be in one piece. The end of the week was fast on him. And he could feel the tension with the screws and certain inmates. Oh, this was gonna be a barrel of laughs.

Grandad finished his book and began to shift weight and jog on the spot. Every now and then he would throw out a half inch punch. These punches only took him all his life to master. He was proficient and always knew they would be needed. He had used said techniques in a Dojo and they had been useful. He knew that any day now he would be needing to use them. It would be a kill or be killed situation and he had been in that predicament once or twice before, once with the law, the other with a bad debt. He waited for night to come and settled into a zen state of mind. One where he was fully at peace but alert at the same time. He knew that this would be tricky, He made a retsu hand shape that was used to keep him in a sharp state off mind and he was totally prepared.

Then it happened. The large Iron door was opened and three of them stepped into the light. The first was the screw and Grandad was taking nae chances. He threw his first punch. The screw flew out the door and hit the railing a crumpled mess. The second one gulped a dry gulp. And began to retreat. The third who was brandishing a chib, well he thought nothing of it and came straight at Grandad. Grandad blocked the man's weapon and used and old Kata kill point and spirit shouting as he did so, he then pushed the knife hand into the man's guts. Ripping his lower intestine right on his Hari point. The power of Kata, which he never failed at, as he was adept at the skills.

The second guy ran down the stairs and went and got more screws. Grandad, well he could do this all night. Beano and Skull laughed at Grandad and the noise knowing that Grandad had been ready for them. They began shouting and bang their tin cups on the doors chanting, "Grandad, Grandad, Grandad!" This went on the majority of the night and grandad gave up knowing that to carry on would just cause more carnage. He surrendered and was cuffed and sent tae Isolation. The motherfucking hole.

He relaxed when they tossed him into the squalid small cell. He turned and spat down the pan, grimaced and realised, well it could be worse. Then he sat in a corner and shivered through his bones. He didn't know how long he was gonna be in there. But after what he had just done it was going to be a while. The screw was sent tae the hospital the other Pet well he died of a burst hernia. The whole jail was buzzing about it. He asked the screws if he could have something to read. They came back with the book cart, Grandad smiled and said, "You got any Hunter S. Thompson" The older gentlemen said, "Aye I got *'Hells Angels'* and I got *'The Rum Diary'*."

Grandad smiled and replied, "I'll hae the two". He opened up *'The Rum Diary'* and a packet of skins fell to the floor. Then a small pouch of baccy landed next tae it. Grandad thanked the old book man. Then rolled one and began tae smoke. Whilst reading *'Hells Angels'*.

CHAPTER 15

Sheila smiled after a quick chat with McCrann. It was looking positive. But just after the conversation he was being summoned into court to answer for the two charges, one was the death of an inmate and subsequent serious assault on a Prison Warder.

"Gail, get my things, he's fucked it up".

Gail sighed and replied, "Yes Mr McCrann".

He then headed for the Sheriff Courts in the centre of Edinburgh. Grandad waited, knowing that he will be straight up in front of the Sheriff. As the crime was a state of self defence and Grandad was just protecting himself, he knew he was in for a shout as the Guard was due to be disciplined for the assault on Grandad. Leon was taken to the holding cells in the bowels of the court building. There he waited until the duty Sargent had finished bringing down two other convicts who had figured they would get away wae light sentencing. But alas no they were put into the holding cell opposite Grandad.

They stood with their mouths open as the Duty Sargent took Grandad away to have a stiff extra sentence hung on him, Grandad didn't give a fuck. He was well on the bright side wae the other inmates. All he had to worry about after all the plea bargaining and showing of evidence to the Sheriff court on how it was duress and Grandad answered, "There were three of them sir".

The Sheriff noted and said after a brief word from the PF. "I'm inclined to let you go but the system is full of lighter sentencing so I will pass down the sentence of and extra three months".

Grandad smiled and replied, "Thank you sir".

The Sheriff waved his hand and the sentence was carried out immediately. Grandad was moved back tae Gen Pop. The whole hall was up in arms celebrating the fact that Grandad had done something that was only the sane thing tae do and that was defend himself. It's just a cold motherfucking fact that he had expert training. The Sheriff knew this of course, but managed to overlook the fact, Grandad could and had been a cold fucking Killer. He revelled in the salutations of the hall. He truly had struck a blow not just for the Y.B.C. but for all the cons in that hall. Grandad rolled over and slept of his crowning achievement. He smiled as the tranny blasted out rock anthems, from Fleetwood Mac to the Stones and a little bit of Indie Oasis *Don't look back in anger I heard you say*.

He slumbered well into the early hours in the morning. He smiled as the door was opened and he went and got his cup of tea and cereal. The whole hall was in a state of calm and that suited Grandad just right. I mean one less corrupt bent screw tae deal wae. Grandad smiled as Beano and Skull came up tae him.

Beano was first to ask, "Who trained you?"

Grandad smiled and replied, "cannea tell you that".

Then Skull put in, "Well those are moves to be admired. I'd gie a king's ransom to learn even a little bit oh your styles."

Grandad smiled and replied, "It took me years to get the technique correct".

Skull sat down and asked, "You must have been born wie a gift like that",

Grandad smiled, "Aye and it was still a nightmare tae learn".

Beano smiled and handed Grandad a bottle full of methadone. "That's tae help wae the cold turkey".

Grandad nodded his head and said, "Thanks man".

Beano walked away to get his breakfast, Skull followed him.

"A king's ransom," he said just as he left. "Well, it aint Tae Kwon Do," he said to Beano then the two of them went and had breakfast.

Grandad left tae go back tae his cell. Grandad still had the two books he got in isolation. And was about half way through *Hell's Angels*.

He spoke a little whilst reading, "A publicity stunt, it just seemed that way surely".

He carried on reading, Hunter S. Thompson was well out of his league with the *Hell's Angels*. But he would give the book it's Gonzo flavour and that was a surprising work of art. He then switched on his tranny and listened to Planet Rock with Alice Cooper. He was enjoying the rock anthems and the discussion he was having about certain songs and music, Grandad drifted to sleep with the tranny playing through-out his nap.

⚜

Pinkie smiled as he returned tae his hoose across fae the shops in Sighthill. He produced skins, fags and a bit if dope. He began tae build a joint. It didn't take long, and he had a nice mellow smoke on his own, He smiled and said to no one, "If it aint broke don't fix it". Then went and got himself a bottle of Budweiser ice. He sat swigging from the bottle and toked his brains out. It was a nice piece of dope and was doing just what it was meant tae do and that was get him high. He reached over tae the phone and dialled Jan's Hoose. It rang out for a few seconds then it was answered.

"Jan here how can I help?" She asked as well whilst she purred at the same time.

Oh, she had her sexy nature nailed tae a T. "It's me Pinkie, is Giz there?"

She smiled and replied, "Aye but shouldn't you be at prayer meeting?"

Pinkie smiled and said, "Nah doll only Sundays".

She smiled then shouted through tae Giz, "Giz your brother the Pope is on the Phone".

Giz laughed and made his way tae the phone. "Awright Pinkie?" He asked then the two of them got down tae brass tacks.

"Grandad blew it," said Pinkie.

Giz smiled and took a draw fae his fag. "It was, self-defence," said Giz.

Pinkie carried on, "He was lucky the Sheriff was generous with him".

Giz smiled again and replied, "Aye well he's lucky he can handle himself if that was anyone else, they'd still be getting rode".

Pinkie snarled "Fucking bent screws". They carried on the conversation knowing that McCrann was doing the best he could tae get Grandad oot. Pinkie hung up the phone after about ten fifteen minutes, sat down and produced his bag o' toot. He then racked up two lines and snorted them post haste. He then squeaked his teeth and let the drug dae it's work. He smiled and wondered if any of the girls wanted a wee party.

He phoned Shirley, she smiled popped some bubble gum and said, "Sure handsome you just want me or dae yae want me to bring a friend?"

Pinkie knew they would have a ball either way, so he said, "Yeah doll bring a friend".

She smiled and carried on chewing her bubble gum and started to wonder who she should invite. She then thought I'll get Angie.

Pinkie waited for a good hour as the two girls made their way to Pinkies Den. They each had a bag full of vodka cocktails and Diamond White bottles.

"Come in Ladies" Came the invitation fae Pinkie and they both got down to rolling joints and drinking. Pinkie smiled, "Did yie hear aboot Grandad?"

They two of them paused and Angela went, "No What aboot Gramps?"

Pinkie shook his head and said, "He killed an inmate and severely damaged a screw. He claims it was self-defence".

Angela sat with her mouth open and gawped. "Youse pair are major smooth as fuck killers".

Pinkie sneered at this, "Yeah, ain't it a trip." He said.

She smiled and carried on rolling herself a joint.

"Speaking of trips Pinkie. How is God?" asked Shirley.

Pinkie looked at her and said, "I'm never gonna hear the end of this".

Shirley smiled and said, "Nope!"

They carried on with their little party. It went on until wee small hours of the morning. They having drank and toked their coke and dope. No there was no better way to salute the streets than a party. And this always ended up with them in between the sheets playing around, getting off on each other. They had made Pinkies night. And also, he was needing to destress from the whole God thing, it really put the willies up Pinkie, especially when his stash was gone, but Nessy brought it round mid-day the next day. He was thankful of that and he told Nessy, "You still owe me fur the beers".

Nessy pulled out a ten-pound note and said, "That'll cover it Mate?"

Pinkie smiled, "Don't ever spook someone like that again".

Nessy laughed then stopped "No! your serious?"

Pinkie grinned a malicious psycho grin and said, "I am serious". He then went back in slamming the door just to accentuate the mood he was in. He walked over to the phone and called hame.

"Awright mam?" He asked as she lifted the phone.

"Aye son, see your pal is up for a severe sentence".

Pinkie smiled and replied, "Och he got off light. And I mean light!"

She lit up a fag and carried on, "I hope you arnea planning to going back inside?"

Pinkie smiled and thought 'Straight tae the point'. But she knew she hadnea raised a couple of wee dafties. She had two crooks fur sons. And in her own kinda way she was well proud of them. I mean she had walked the way through when Jan was beaten and raped. She had kept herself sane knowing that Giz was head over heels in love wae her, it didnea matter that she was a druggie and a femme fatale. This only made her son stronger. And Grandad well she was going tae have words wae him herself when he got oot about friendship and all that was around the term friends. She felt let doon by the laddie.

Pinkie had a long conversation saying that Grandad was one of the better ones. He kept in contact and shared the booty, this was why she had come to the solution of just talking tae him. But it would wait, Grandad was swinging the Gallows pole and having a good time o' it. Like I said earlier he was like royalty to most folk. Had saved a lot of necks, including Pinkie and Gizmos. Which was, by all accounts, a Godsend, as Pinkie had only been out a couple of months and knew if he landed the wrong side of the law it would be a life sentence. And that was twenty-one years, hard time.

The finished talking and Grandad was never mentioned during the whole conversation. Pinkie hung up and went and bought a nice small French lager twenty-four pack. He loaded the lager into the fridge and left it there. For a good hour just enough to give it a frosty chill. Then he popped the cap and sat back and drank. He was in heaven this night could'nea get any better. He rolled a spliff and sat and blazed away. Then he went and put on some music, Pink Floyd *Wish you were Here*. Giz landed at his door about the same time as the sun went down. Pinky laughed as the thought *Shining On* was a great idea. Giz smiled at the half-cut brother of his. Pinkie let him in. Giz produced a bag of Eckies. Twenty in total. Pinkie smiled and carried on drinking.

"Can I hae ane?" Giz asked Pinkie, Pinkie smiled and replied, "Aye man you ken where the fridge is".

Giz helped himself. He came back through and handed Pinkie a sweetie, a dancing sweetie. They were rhubarbs and custards. And were priceless. The rush built up and the two of them were in happy hard-core heaven. They changed the music tae Underworlds, *Second Toughest in the Infants*. The next song tae come on was *Spoonman* then *Kiteless*. 'I see Elvis, And I hear God on the phone. Porn dogs sniffing the wind sniffing the wind for something violent they can do', then they were really rocking. Giz smiled and gleamed through the mad ecstasy. His body jerking and popping to the music. They then after that album they put on another Underworld classic *Beucoup Fish*.

King of Snakes was the best song on the album. They maintained a constant state of Munted. The night reeled on until three four in the morning. At which time they felt the come down. And went to sleep. They woke up starving and Giz dived across tae the bakers tae get a couple o' bacon rolls two each. They ate then went back tae sleep.

CHAPTER 16

Grandad smiled as he woke up, the day was only beginning and Grandad was well, well he was despondent, and knew he had to sign up fur a job, if not anything else but to keep his baccy going. He got a job first in the kitchen then in the laundry. It was only the price of a half-ounce o' baccy a day but that kept him sane. And he sometimes git himself a bag of kit. And got himself a set of works, that he used like twice a week. This was a substance of choice and the methadone programme was a Godsend. It took the edge of it, his habit was pretty much under control, but he knew he had a long time tae go. The screw that he had damaged was vowing revenge. Grandad he was easy about it and Beano and Skull were keeping an eye on him. He was safe as could be for the moment. He carried on reading the two books that he had procured fae the library. He finished them and got himself some Kerouac and Bukowski. Then after filling his mind with them he moved onto a stone-cold classic *Junkie*. The William Burroughs set-u-straight about habits and how tae kick them. He read the book three four times knowing that it would put you straight about junk. He smiled and carried on reading. Liam would be proud of him knowing that those books were on high demand in the Tin Pail. Especially Junkie. He made a note tae himself and that was tae get a copy of Junkie as soon as he was released.

He also sampled poetry by Ginsberg, knowing that him Burroughs and Kerouac were practically joined at the hip. Grandad was becoming quite the bookworm.

He carried on reading Ginsberg then fell into a slight Gouch and sleep. A couple of days later after finishing *On the Road* Grandad wondered whether he would ever get to see America, probably not though. He smiled and carried on his junk induced slumber. He woke at around tea-time and headed fur his dinner. He ate and ate heartily, the meal was a treat that night, a sausage roll, some scabby chips and some beans. Once he was done and free he would definitely be calling a chinkie. He kept this in mind and it was a constant source of comfort that he would be free and he would be out and living it up again. He made plans whilst inside it was what was keeping him sane.

Several months fell of the Calandar and he had been in contact with his brief who was always saying positive stuff like the Appeal was finalised and that it wouldn't be long until they had a date for his appeal. A couple of months. He smiled he could be getting a release in a about six months. This was all he needed tae hear. He smiled and carried on reading *'The Big Sur'* by Jack Kerouac. It was a good novel unto which Kerouac was having a minor schizophrenic breakdown he laughed and said; "I'd rather be a shitty person any day rather that than go through the paranoid trip that he was undergoing. He smiled and thought I must be privileged. As he read on, he felt more and more sorry for the character. He then finished the book and thought 'paranoid!' and that was putting it mildly. The book was like a bad trip on acid and it got more intense as it got further through. Grandad smiled oh to be a schizophrenic in the USA. 'I suppose it would have its own charms'.

Grandad turned over after lights out and fell into a sleep. A sleep haunted by noises of waves and paranoid waffling of sex gone wrong and bad drugs. Particularly when he had realised, he had emptied the rat poison and killed the poor mouse, he woke the next morning smiled and tossed the book aside 'Finished'. He thought 'Thank fuck'. I mean it was entertaining, but it was also strong on the paranoid delusional side something he didn't plan on getting. No, the lot of them the whole literary pack well they were obviously insane. Burroughs had killed his wife playing William Tell with a thirty-eight revolver. It was amazing to see that justice was just that fucked up over there. He smiled and headed tae the shower room. "Thank God I'm Scottish," he said then carried on cleaning himself. After breakfast he was back in the laundry room. Beano approached him wae a bag o' kit.

Grandad smiled and said, "Cheers pal"/ Grandad carried on his work, then lunch, then he readied himself another shot of heroin. It was becoming a regular thing and he knew himself that he was getting to be a chronic abuser of Skag. But he had given up on the mentality of self-abuse and torturing himself. It got him nowhere and nowhere fast, But still he held on, still he waited for the sentence to be reduced. His Attorney was making great head way, providing that he kept his nose clean. This was going to be a hard job after the Screw, he was beginning to be more hassle as the screws pets came at him and they came at him hard and right when he was at his weakest. That was whilst he was withdrawing from junk. But it was still easier for him than you thought.

He was still practicing Martial arts and still they kept coming. I mean the screw had some balls on him and wasn't going to quit. He was working out in the rec room and keeping in shape and Skag, well it was a natural painkiller and took the pain away. He found he only needed to Inject every second day. Grandad slept with one eye open. Then suddenly there was a drought of smack in the jail. And that was when the screw got up the guts to try again. This time he would wait in his cell after he finished in the laundry room. Grandad walked in and was grabbed as soon as he entered his cell. The next two hours was the worst pain he had ever endured. They beat and raped him for an hour solid. They left him with a nasty scar along his cheek, and he was withdrawing fae the smack. This was only a mild discomfort as he was again in the Infirmary. But you think he would roll over and complain. No but it left him messed up. He vowed to get them one by one. There were four of them and they took their time and made sure he felt every minute of the beating and agonizing rape. He again got privileges, extra visit's fae family. His mam took one look at the state of him and was shocked and horrified. She stifled a scream and Sheila looked deep into his eyes and said, "Now you really have a beef".

Grandad looked away the steel in his eyeballs glaring and stark. He would hope that he got out soon. Then vengeance then payback. She laughed and Grandad made himself comfortable.

"Oh, that scar really sets your eyes off", she said he smiled a little. Knowing full and well what she meant. This was personal. I mean four of them including the screw. "Your Brief will have a field day when he sees you".

Grandad smiled again. Beano popped in to visit him whilst he was recuperating. He could hear the whole jail close tae rioting. The three convicts were released a day or two later. The screw couldn't have been more proud of his action. And Grandad got back to the cell after ten days in the Jail hospital. His Brief was assuring him that everything was being held instead of his case and that it could only swing in his favour. He smiled and noticed there was a book on his bed *Fear and Loathing in Las Vegas*. Hunter S. Thompson' He smiled there was a bookmark with the words "Fae Beano and Skull".

He smiled and dived right into the book. No time like the present. He was then officially being released in two weeks. He was straight onto the blower speaking tae Pinkie. Pinkie knew the script and knew it well. But Grandad was growling after the call, thinking Mr Rafferty (The Screws name) I'll deal wae you personally. He then got on the blower and Spoke tae Kingo.

Kingo smiled and said, "Watcha want Gramps.?"

Grandad replied, "I need a favour".

Kingo laughed. "Straight back tae Business".

Grandad growled, "Nah man this is personal".

Kingo laughed, "Oh I bet it is".

"We'll meet in a week or so," continued Grandad. Pinkie went straight back tae his den after picking some money up fae Grandad's Uncle, Doughnut.

He then began tae organize a freedom party. Grandad was out three days later. In which he was picked up by Pinkie, who for his sins was driving a Volkswagen Golf. He sat there as it was the Middle of winter and fucking freezing. Grandad got in and Pinkie smiled looking at the scar on his cheek.

"Biscuit wants a word," said Pinkie.

Grandad's face was stoney and sour, "We'll make him first port of call."

Pinkie laughed and said, "It suits you, both the tattoo and the scar".

Grandad went quiet and answered after a couple of seconds, "Thanks man".

They then headed up tae Biscuit's. First thing Biscuit did was size him up. He then turned his cheek and ran his finger down his cheek and said, "Join the club". Grandad laughed and biscuit smiled.

"Anything you need, anything at all just ask".

Grandad smiled, "I could murder a bottle of beer".

Biscuit walked over tae the mini fridge and produced a Bud Ice.

Grandad sat down and popped the cap. He took a swig and went, "Ahhh that's better than good".

Biscuit and Grandad spraffed for at least an hour. Gramps showed him the Joker tattoo. And Biscuit was impressed.

Then after a while Pinkie was getting anxious. So, he said tae Gramps, "we got angels tae meet".

Grandad smiled the grin that could win, and he and Pinkie headed across the way tae their den. They parked the Golf and into the Den they went.

Pinkie said, "you wanna a Chinese?"

Grandad puffed on a ready rolled joint and said, "I've been dreaming o' a chinky".

Pinkie smiled, "I take it it's the usual lemon chicken, fried rice and salt and pepper ribs."

Grandad smiled then said, "Aye man, when are the girls due?"

"Oh, they'll be a while as they, you know have to put there Lippy on and that".

"How many and who?" asked Gramps.

Pinkie smiled, "Four or five, you want I'll phone Tequila?"

Grandad Laughed and said, "I better phone her".

Pinkie sat down and said Chinkies on its way. Then Grandad picked up the phone and dialled Sheila.

"Aye doll, no doll come if you want". He smiled and relaxed, "She's on her way".

Pinkie smiled and Grandad asked, "You gonna phone your brother?"

Pinkie stood up "Oh shit Giz and Jan". Then he phoned her house in which Giz was having a shower and getting ready to step oot. "I didnea tell him you were oot today".

Grandad smiled and said. "You better hurry, coz they will probably be planning tae go oot."

Pinkie was on the phone about a quarter hour squaring things wae Giz.

"Why did you no tell me he was oot the day?"

Pinkie smiled and thought, 'I'm regretting it now',

Then he hung up and carried in getting everything ready for the company they were about tae hae. He tossed Grandad an eckie. It was a Fiori and was a nice E tae snort. Sheila was first tae arrive and Pinkie invited her in, she was carrying a bag full of Diamond White and a couple bottles of Lambrusco. And enough ganja it would have made a Rasta's brain water.

Grandad got down rae brass tacks and started to roll a large cone. He packed the thing and handed the lump of dope back tae Tequila. Then he began tae sink a Bud Ice. She kissed his cheek in particular his new-found scar. Then as the joint was smoking and smoking well the rest of them began tae join the party. Angie, Shirley, Hazel, Vikki Gregg and a few others. The house was bouncing with House of Pain playing in the background. *Same as it ever was* the whole block was bouncing. The neighbours even joined in though they weren't too sure what they were celebrating. Just joined in the fun, I mean what the hell, what else were they gonna do. I mean it was something you couldn't avoid.

The Polis arrived and knew straight away who was being toasted.

"Grandad," they said then turned around and left. Knowing that they could'nea dae nothing to the guy. Grandad sat back pure buzzing if the E's and dope. Grandad pulled Pinkie aside and said, "We got business to discuss".

Pinkie smiled, "Aye, aye, that wae dae".

Grandad was obviously in the mood for a spraf about getting revenge. "The conversation was taut yet to the point. Grandad's face was chiselled and impassive. He was totally in the Zone and wanted tae make plans tae get back at that bent fucking screw and all his pets. They had a good hour discussing how they were going tae get the bent screw.

Grandad knew that Kingo would be the best tae get an address. Pinkie agreed and said I'll get Giz, then he shouted on Giz tae come over. Gizmo stopped his conversation wae the tall dark horny lass, he excused himself and went over tae Pinkie and Grandad.

"Awright lads?" He asked then sat down.

Grandad sneered and started to lay down his plan. He was fucking positive that the screw and his pets weren't getting away with it. He knew that Beano and Skull would take care of the pets that were still inside and Grandad would make sure that the screw well, Grandad thought about it and it was the best idea to give him a Chelsea. Grandad looked over at the front door and saw Kingo arrive just as the conversation was tapering off.

"Kingo!" He shouted and Kingo smiled and walked over to the three of them. Kingo looked over at Grandad's face "Was that as sare as it looks?"

Gramps smiled through the scar. And replied, "Aye sare as it looks", Came the reply fae Gramps.

Pinkie smiled as the two of them began to spraff about revenge. Kingo was sure he could get the Screws address. And that suited Grandad down tae the ground. They carried on until about five or six in the morning and the booze and the E's had worn off.

Grandad headed up the road wae his arm and jacket around Tequila. Keeping her close and comfortable. It had been a wild party and all Grandad wanted tae dae was relax wae his woman. He unlocked the door and before they even got across the doorway, they began tae neck. He had missed this so much whilst he was inside. They went through the bedroom peeling of each other's clothes. They were down tae their underwear by time they got tae the bed. Immediately grandad got down tae business.

He slid down her body and pushed his face between her legs and began the best part of sex, oral. Then they slipped between the sheets and got into the position that they were most comfortable with sixty-nine. Grandad smiled as her warm sweet smell engulfed him, her wetness, her amber pubic hair. And he carried on in this position until they were both satisfied. Then she went on top. Grandad loved her breasts whilst she rode him cowgirl style and they both orgasmed at the same time. Then they had about ten minutes at mutual masturbation, which was classed as after play. But the two of them had been holding on for about a year and three months. They then fell into a contented sleep, both of them very satisfied.

Grandad lit up a fag after a long-contented sleep. He smiled and sighed and looked over the body of his lover she was smiling in her slumber and that made all the difference. He sighed a heartfelt sigh. With dawn approaching and the light filtering into the bedroom. Giving the room a golden glow and everything was pristine. Grandad sighed again and took another draw from his fag. Tequila woke about half an hour later. She smiled looked at him and said, "Hi handsome".

Grandad nodded and replied, "Hi tae you tae".

They lay and smoked a couple of fags then got up and got on with their day. Lorna smiled and shouted through to the two of them, "How are my two love birds?"

Sheila smiled and replied, "Aye Lorna we're just fine".

Lorna smiled. "I'll get breakfast on the go".

Grandad relaxed a little bit more and said, "Aye breakfast".

⚜

Giz and Pinkie headed tae their mam's House, Jan was on Giz's arm and Shirley was on Pinkies. They turned the road that was where their parents lived. It was eight o'clock in the morning and they were still half cut fae the night before. They all staggered slightly. Then Giz produced the key tae the door. He unlocked it whilst fumbling at the same time. This woke their mum up, who immediately started to rain on their parade.

"I take it he's oot, He here wae yies?" Pinkie laughed.

"Nah mam he's at his mams wae Sheila".

Cathie who obviously needed a Valium snarled at the pair of them. "Well, the moment he arrives you send him through tae me. I want words wae the creep".

Pinkie and Giz sent the two girls through to their room. They began to spliff up and drank a little Lambrusco. Cathie was still no finished she was reading the two brothers the riot act. They still wurnea sure what it was that Grandad had done to deserve the wrath of their mother and they knew it must have been serious.

"Mam, mam, he's just oot the Jail, he needs time tae adjust".

She sneered again, "That's just the problem everyone has to walk on fucking eggshells when he is around, well nae mare I want a word in his ear? So soon as he arrives you tell me and me and that laddie are going tae have a chat" Gizmo looked at his brother and said in a low whispering tone. "Let's grab the girls and go up tae Jans".

Pinkie nodded and Their mam finished the argument. She then went and had a cup of tea in the kitchen. The four o' them left and headed up tae Westburn where Jan was now housed.

Shirley who was still surprised that they didnea cross words wae her said, "What did Grandad dae tae warrant your mams wrath?"

Pinkie just shrugged his shoulders and went, "I dunno".

They then arrived at Jan's pad, the party carried on with just the four of them. They got super high and super drunk. The stone being a mellow one, and they were absolutely sloshed.

⚜

Beefy was way behind on collecting the tick lists that he had four lists in total with five punters per list. He let oot a sigh as if this was hassle, he didnea need, but someone had to do this part and he knew sure as fuck if he asked someone else, they would fuck it up. On his way to the Sighthill flats he was stopped by Wolfy. Naebody had seen Wolfy in weeks and Beefy didnea like that. He was one of the mob that took nae shit fae anyone. Him Reido, Fabe, Damian Aitken, Banjo and Davey Moss. They were a law unto themselves and naebody could take that away fae them.

Wolfy smiled as Beefy noticed him. "Awright Beefy?" said Wolfy.

"Where have you been hiding?" Asked Beefy.

Wolfy smiled and said, "Oh I've been dodging around, avoiding the Bizzies".

Beefy nodded his head, "aye well you've missed all the chronic gear".

Wolfy smiled at him as he said this, "Are you holding Beefy?"

Beefy didnea trust the guy as he was known to take liberties. You know take tick then disappear as soon as the time tae pay was around.

Beefy smiled, "Nah man you missed all the Chronic stuff!"

Wolfy sighed and said, "That's too bad as I was going tae pay straight away".

Beefy smiled, "let's see some colour then Wolfy?"

Wolfy produced a fat wallet with tens and twenties.

Beefy produced a bag of Northern Lights Grass, some E's Mitsies and Fioris. "I got smack tae".

Wolfy smiled and said, "how much?"

Beefy smiled and said, "Fiver a gramme fur the Grass, sixty for ten eckies, and a tenner a bag for the Horse".

Wolfy smiled, "What kinda kit is it?"

Beefy smiled at him, "It's Indian candy," he said.

Then Wolfy started to count out the money. "That's six gramme of Grass, twenty E's, Ten o' each and four bags o' smack".

Beefy showed him into the stairwell and began to produce the narcotics. Then they shook on it and Wolfy handed over the cash. 'It was meant tae be' thought Beefy then he went and collected the rest of his tick lists. Wolfy smiled and walked away heading tae Banjo's. Knowing that, that was a proper result when it went that smoothly.

⚜

Cha heard what happened tae Grandad in the Jail and got right on the blower tae his Compadre, Raymie, who was just of the phone wae Biscuit who had just filled him in on the details, Raymie began to speak tae Cha and told him what he already knew, "Grandad was tanned and they made him their Bitch for a couple of hours."

Cha snarled at both the statement and the fact he already knew. He then said, "I ken this".

Raymie smiled "it's about tae get messy again".

Cha carried on the conversation, "aye that's what they pay us the big bucks for. I'll hau tae phone Grandad see how he is wanting tae handle this".

Cha then hung up and straight away called Grandad.
"Hello Gratton household?"

Cha smiled, "Aye Lorna it's Leon's pal Charlie. Is Leon around?"

She smiled "Aye sweety, I'll just go and get him".

She then went through smiling her teeth out. "Leon It's a Charlie on the phone for you."

Grandad got up and went and spoke, "Awright Cha?"

Cha smiled and said, "Aye man, heard what happened in the Tombs!"

Grandad smiled and said, "It's okay I'm fine",

Cha went off his head, "I'm no accepting that. You know the script, if they harm one of us, they harm all of us",

Grandad was stunned tae the fact of silence. "Aye I ken Cha. But I'm bidding my Time".

Cha whistled to stop him from whining on, Gramps shot a steely glare out into nowhere.

"Okay Cha, the moment I've got the Screws address I'll take you and Raymie wae me and we'll fix him good style".

Cha sighed and said, "That's better Gramps, that's more like the top boy you're suppose tae be".

He then hung up. Cha smiled and went and got himself a Tenent's lager. He was watching the Edinburgh Old firm Clash Hibs versus Hearts. He should have went but knew that HBC and the CCS were at their pinnacle, which was just the way things were going down. They were creaming Hearts on and off the pitch. The CSF were poor at the meets and Cha couldn't see them getting any better. He pulled the ring pull on his can took a big fucking gulp practically emptying the can in a oner'. He smiled as Hibs were all over Hearts. And the Game had just started.

CHAPTER 17

Grandad slipped back into the sheets with Sheila they began to fool around and giggle. Grandad was right where he wanted to be and that was as close to heaven as you could get without dying. He went throughout the day smiling and exploring her as did she with him. They made each other complete. And needed nothing else other than each other. It was heavenly and they didn't need to relax around each other they were in a perfect state of calm and the little else they did was well defined in a pure state of substance. Nothing was what they needed and no one else could change them. Bjork was playing on the radio the song *Venus as a Boy*. It was a subtle song aimed primarily at lovers, especially loving tender boys that took their time in bed. And girls love that. Like the song said, 'As venus as a boy, 'He touches, they carried on, nodding off occasionally in each-others, arms.

⚜

Gizmo and Pinkie were carrying on with their dope session, smiling as they kissed and toked with the two girls. Shirley sat back, popped a bubble from her bubble gum and took several tokes, of the joint and smiled as Pinkie crawled into her arms and they began to neck and spoon each other. Their hands moving around their erogenous zones stroking and getting heavier and heavier the girls were wet and both Gizmo and pinkie were hard. They needed no formal invite, so they began to fuck their partners and the four of them got down and dirty. Gizmo loved Janice and she loved him. They were seldom apart these days. And it suited the two of them down tae a T. He had saved her life and she loved him for it, he was fast at falling in love wae her. It was a beautiful set up and they had each other, right where they wanted each other. And their passion, it would set the world on fire. They were equal in their ways and smiling everyday. It was one of those things that had caused them much pleasure. And it was beautiful tae watch. And everyone said so.

Grandad rolled some more in the hay wae Tequila. They were also beautiful to watch. They were passionate and tender at the same time. It was an art form itself and nobody could dispute that. They could hold themselves together like glue they were so on each-others wavelength. The day turned to night and they were in the throes of passion.

⚜

Kingo walked from the underpass fae a spraf wae Squeak and Legs. He knew that the time for action was imminent. He got hold of his contact PC Anderson. He was only a flat foot, but he came up with the goods. That included stolen narcotics on the day it was due to be incinerated, the substances just vanished, nobody knew it was him. Figuring him to be a straight cut man. He even slipped out a couple of keys of coke for Kingo.

Kingo spoke tae the guy, "Where does the screw Rafferty stay?

PC Steven Anderson began to complain. "

Shush you flat foot, you're in my pocket pal," said Kingo,

Steve wondered if he would ever be better off. "Not fucking likely," he said out loud.

Kingo went, "Huh what did you say?"

Steven cursed himself then gave Kingo the right answer "I'll have it in two days".

Kingo smiled and then said "And I want his pets as well?"

Steve smiled and went through the motions "Yes Willie. No Willie".

Kingo hung up on the guy, abruptly so. Then walked away whistling, his part in this was just starting and he loved acts of war. Especially on the system.

⚜

Pinkie and Giz walked hame fae Jans. The two of them covered in love bites on their necks and chests. They got to the front door and Cathie, their mum, was straight at the two of them. "Where is he? You promised you would let me have words wae him?"

Pinkie smiled a goofy loved up tanked on ecstasy smile, "chill out mom," he said.

Giz punched him one on the arm and hissed, "we are hame daftie!"

Pinkie stopped and realised that he wasn't up to smoozing her no, he had to think survival, "Aye well yie see he's at hame".

He stopped and wondered where the beautiful butterfly came fae. It was circling his head and making him translucent. Giz had decided tae got to his bed. James was well still wondering about the beautiful butterfly. His mam gave up and went through the kitchen. She stood and had a fag, Pinkie well he was chasing faeries. He stopped and thought, I better get some sleep. Then straight through to the room and onto the top bunk. He was spacing out yet calm, as nothing was going to change him from his silky sleep. Giz was snoring five seconds after his head hit the pillow. Cathie was having a small bubble. Her eyes welling up, she began to count her blessings, she was lucky that neither of her sons were dead. She missed Shimmey and Shimmey was well he was missed by everyone. She stopped herself and laughed. At least Broomie is top of the toon. Then wiped her eyes dry and went through and started her new book a Stephen King novel, *Dreamcatcher.* The boys rested.

⚜

Grandad woke tae his house phone ringing. Kingo had got the address o' the screw. Grandad growled as he wrote down the address, "Cheers Kingo".

Kingo smiled and went, "Nae bother Gramps" He then went through and slipped back next tae Tequila. He rested and smoked a fag. Sheila was giving of a gentle noise, which reminded him a' her experiments with Dildos. That was all part of the flavour with Tequila, that and she was quirky and hyper at times. Especially when it came to criminal activities. And feeling the fear then doing it. She was an abstract beauty with a personality that shone radiance. And she could pull tricks and stunts.

Grandad knew some day they would settle, but just now he was in the midst of war. He had everything tae prove. That it was not just the scar that he was angry about, no he was angry about the whole scenario the length they took to make his time a misery. Three hours they kept him there. Buttfucking him, he sat and scowled at the thoughts he still had and decided to get up before he blew his stack. He went through to the kitchen, his mam sat there having a fag.

"You okay son?"

He smiled but couldn't say anything nice. "Fucking bastarding fucking Jail. Has left a scar on me and don't just mean a wound I mean a scar that will always be there".

His mum smiled a small smile and said, "Time heals all wounds".

Grandad laughed and said, "I know Mam, where would I be without your pearls of wisdom?" He sat down and had a fag and a cup o' tea. He smiled and talked a while. Sheila came through wearing his best Nirvana T-shirt, the *Nevermind* one with Kurt swimming wae his axe in the pool. She smiled and sat down produced a regal and they all smoked their little hearts out. Grandad went through and changed into his togs including Addidas trainers and Addidas top. And Peppe Jeans. He put on his Fred Perry jacket and said, "I'm awa oot tae see Cha and Raymie". Sheila put on some Finlay Quaye and hung about the hoose. Lorna got on with the stairs and lifts. It was a charming job, Piss all over the stairwell and puddle's o piss in the lifts. But she got tae live in the flat rent free. And her phone bills were taking care of.

CHAPTER 18

Grandad met up wae Cha at Misfits. Cha stood up as soon as he saw Gramps, he walked over and they gripped wrists. Then Grandad went and got himself a bottle of German Heiniken lager. Cha smiled as he took his seat.

"Where's Raymie?" asked Grandad. Cha smiled a wicked smile and said, "He'll be along later".

Grandad smiled.

Cha continued, "it's quarter tae one he'll be sleeping off last night".

Grandad smiled and said, "Kingo is on it, I should have his address by the middle of next week".

Cha smiled and poured himself another lager. "Aye like I said Gramps. You cannae let the guy away wae it."

Grandad lit up a fag. Then Cha, looked at his scar and said, "It suits you five skinner".

Grandad looked away not wanting to appear hurt. "Aye Cha a five stitcher".

Cha laughed. "Well, all the girls say it sets your eyes ablaze" Gramps laughed a small humph. "You got tae look at the positive, there is always a positive side tae everything".

Grandad stood up and headed back tae the bar. He got himself a jug o' Tennent's and two shots of Tequila one fur Cha and one fur himself. He sat back down and Cha lit up a spliff. That's when Raymie arrived. He looked at Gramps in particular the scar he smiled and said, "A fiver skinner huh".

Raymie sat down and Cha handed him the joint. Raymie puffed in the doobie and they began to relax and spraf. The session went on for a good five six hours. Cha was having a discussion about wee Dawn. Apparently, she had got in contact to see if there was any hope for her getting back wae Grandad, she left very disappointed. Cha broke it as subtlety as he could. Knowing she was very much in love wae Grandad. He hated it just messed wae everyone's head.

He told her, "Hold on there doll, silver lining. You know there's always light at the end of the tunnel".

She smiled a wee smile and headed hame. Grandad felt fur her, really felt fur her. But him and Tequila well they were practically married. The conversation rattled on most o' the night. Grandad was telling the tale about Beano and Skull. And how the majority of the Tombs were on his side. I mean he was practically royalty in some of their eyes. To others he was like an apostle. Grandad took note and stayed in the warmth of their worship. I mean the tattoo and he showed the pair them the stick thin tatt of the Joker holding a smoking gun in a purple and green suit.

"How much did that cost?" asked Raymie.

Grandad smiled and replied, "It was fucking free".

Cha smiled and returned, "See that's the thing you make all the right moves and they set you free. And I don't just mean Jail time, I mean everyone has your best interest at heart". He then grabbed Grandad and planted one in his scarred cheek.

"Luvly. You've never done anything that was not luvly". Raymie went tae the bar and ordered A jug each o' Tennants. Grandad finished his last one just as Raymie brought two to him and Cha. Then he went back and got his. They finished sometime later. Grandad jumped into a taxi and went hame tae Tequila. She was sitting in his room listening tae Bob Dylan. With a spliff and a bottle o' diamond white. He staggered in and she looked at him and said, "Hello Handsome?"

Grandad smiled and replied, "Hello Darlin!"

She walked over tae him and grabbed him by the neck and began tae kiss him, Grandad was not surprised by the action as they were really going hot and heavy. And it was take no prisoners time. They fell into bed and fell more in love. Grandad was a satisfied man knowing he had made all the right moves.

Kingo smiled and wrote down the address of the Screw. PC Anderson really came through with the goods. He took down the address that was in the Currie area of Edinburgh, just off the Pentland hills. He smiled and said, "and when is he up for a shift.?

"Tomorrow, he leaves his house at seven thirty in the morning". Kingo wrote down the address smiled and said, "I'll make this one up tae yae".

PC Anderson sighed and said, "Aye well some of that profit that you all get would be nice?"

Kingo smiled again, "Aye Steve, fur this one I'll cut you a slice".

He hung up and went and got a hold o' his contact list and phoned Pinkie who rose twice, once to have a Jews wish and the other, well he was drinking some sort of liquid that turned out tae be shampoo. His mum rushed him into A and E. He was in the back o' the motor blowing bubbles out his mouth and gurgling like a bairn. He could swear he ate a melon as-well. Nope that was a bar o' soap. They pumped his stomach and it was just as well his mother had heard him choking.

On the road to the Hospital his mum was shouting at him, "Stupid, stupid, boy, Stupid, stupid, stupid boy. He woke an hour later starving. His mam sat there and watched as he came out of his unconscious state.

"You stupid, stupid, boy you could have died".

Pinkie sat up and said "Mam?" Cathie was really raging at him, "What she returned?" Pinkie grinned at her, "I'm starving." She couldn't help but laugh, She went and got him a sandwich fae the shop.

"BLT", he said as she handed him the sandwich. He smiled and all she could see was the funny side o' it.

Grandad landed at Kingo's door about ten am and rapped on his door. Kingo answered about two minutes later, "Awright Gramps?"

Grandad smiled and put out his hand. Kingo put a piece of paper with the address on it. "he's on day shift all week so your best chance is early in the morning".

Gramps smiled then walked away. Not saying a word. He was really buzzed about the whole situation. He felt a little rushed into the action but knew that this was the only way he would get results. He got home and dialled Cha.

"Aye Cha, it's me Gramps".

Cha started to laugh at how long it took Grandad tae come up wae the address. "I told you Cha it isnea a problem. I just wanted to make sure that the guy wusnea suspicious o' us",

Cha laughed again,

"Anyway," said Grandad. "I'm gonna carve my name on the cunt".

Cha stopped laughing and replied, "Thats mare like it Grandad".

Grandad smiled a malicious grin. "Two days and we'll be on target, wae the cunt."

Cha snarled down the phone and said, "I like hard talk Grandad".

The two of them went back tae their business. He just had tae make sure that Grandad was serious.

⚜

Pinkie finished his sandwich and started to drink a bottle of Lucozade, He was absolutely thirsty and starving. His mam sat there totally fuming wae her boy.

"You could have died. James".

Pinkie smiled and said, "Dinea worry I'll no be daen that twice".

She blew out a short breath. "You and your brother are always drunk an stoned and I know that the two o' you take drugs, but please, please can you no rocket through your life. I wanna see Grandkids James".

Pinkie saddened by the whole spiel smiled and said, "I'll try mam, I'll try". A tear ran down his cheek and Pinkie smiled a sad soft smile. His mam really was trying tae reach oot tae him. He fell back asleep and she watched then left when visiting hours ended. Grandad got right on the phone tae Gizmo, Gizmo picked up and said, "Hello".

Grandad replied, "Giz, It's me Grandad".

Giz told him that his brother was in hospital after swallowing a bubble. Grandad winced slightly at the thought o' him drinking shampoo.

"He okay?"

Gizmo let out a wee chuckle,

"Aye they pumped his stomach and gave him a dose o' antacids". Grandad smiled and said, "Close call". Grandad smiled some more, then told Giz the script wae the screw.

Giz smiled and said, "Well I'm up for a wee bit of revenge".

Grandad smiled and said, "That's good Giz, as I'm about tae get really messy" Grandad hung up and got back down tae his lunch.

⚜

Pinkie snarled and carried on defending himself from the onslaught his dad was firing at him. "Aye Da, Aye Da",

His dad was taking no prisoners. "And I tell you something else boy, you are gonna quit this life of intoxication. You will come out clean. You will get a job and you will not end up in prison again!" Pinkie smiled a small sad smile. His dad had made his point and yes, he saw reason. But he had things to tie up loose ends. The argument carried on a full fifteen minutes. Then Big James decided that was enough and left. Pinkie reached for his clothes and decided that he was leaving. I mean it wasn't as if he was terminally ill or anything. He got in a taxi and headed tae Grandads.

⚜

Grandad stood at the door tae haw a smoke, he usually didn'ea bother about the smoke in the house but he needed the fresh air. Pinkie landed at Grandad's door just as he was finishing his fag,

Grandad laughed a small laugh. "Awright Pinkie?" asked Grandad. "What's this I hear that you have taken to clean the hairs inside you?"

Pinkie smiled, "Aye I was wasted".

Grandad beckoned him in tae his hoose. "That's Eckies fur yae", continued Gramps. "Next time check, the bottle. You could have died".

Pinkie sneered uncomfortably. "Just had this mad huge thirst".

Grandad laughed again, "Between you talking tae God then going and trying to see the big man himself, well you're a fucking mess".

Pinkie laughed again, "Aye so my dad is fond of reminding me".

Grandad handed him a joint and said, "take this fur later".

Pinkie pocketed the joint and relaxed. "Have you got any word on where that fucking screw is?"

Grandad nodded his head, "Aye Pinkie, aye, I've got his address, and when he leaves for work".

Pinkie sneered a Sicilian sneer the hate pure in his eyes. Like Cha had said, "you hurt one of us you hurt all of us,"

Grandad sniffed, "I take it that you'll be wanting some blow?"

Pinkie nodded his head and said. "Aye man that would be aces."

Grandad reached into his stash and pulled a bag o' rock. "How much dae yie want?"

Pinkie smiled and said. "Three gramme".

Grandad got the pans out and weighed out three gramme.

Pinkie smiled, "So when is the day of desolation?"

Grandad smiled and slapped the three gramme into his hand. "Day after tomorrow, you cool?"

Pinkie nodded and they gripped wrists. Then Pinkie left. And Grandad carried on his day.

⚜

Tequila smiled as she finished cutting the cocaine she had got from her lover. She squealed as the phone rang; she was having a good day. It was Grandad.

"Hello lover boy?" she purred as she listened tae her lover.

"Aye doll you hear what happened tae Pinkie?"

She smiled and laughed, "Yeah I heard He's okay now though?"

Gramps snorted a small laugh and replied, "Aye his dad and mum both read him the riot act".

Sheila smiled and returned, "He was wasted I take it, it wusnea an attempt at suicide?"

Grandad smiled, "Nah doll, he was completely wasted thought he was drinking Orange, juice. Didn't even realise he was in the bathroom".

They both had a fit o' the giggles. "I told him tae check the bottle next time".

They both laughed again. "Shampoo reaches the parts where dandruff can't reach," said Grandad.

They both giggled at this. They both left each other knowing that the fact and the fact is shit happens.

⚜

Pinkie smiled and headed hame. He entered and his mum and dad, who were very put out by this whole thing. Well, they had had an argument about Pinkie. He walked in and his mam and dad's bedroom door shut as Big James was seeking solitude. And had had enough of the whole affair. His mam was doing a puzzle book and having a nice cup o' tea. James went straight into the bedroom he shared wae his brother Giz. Giz was oot punting the nice bit o' black he had procured. He kept looking over his shoulder as he had a feeling that things were about tae go tits up again. But he trusted his paranoia as it had served him well the last two wars. He never needed back up 'cause he could slip in and out the areas meeting up wae people who were eager tae score especially the gear that he had. Soft Black gold seal. It was a nice buzz o' gear and came in at a fiver a gramme but that was a gramme bang on. Anything over was classed as a Sixteenth (Sickie) as it was the building games favourite smoke.

People were always wanting more, more, more. He was popular on the street and had already sold a good three four ounce cut and weighed. Business was good and the profits in the game were well, exhausting. Giz never needed for anything, everything took care of everything else. He had a fat pocket and a den that he shared with Pinkie and Grandad. He was the man o' the hour. The connection to have. He had made enough profit to live comfortably and knew he was always on the verge of greatness. He did miss certain people 'Shimmey and Liam' and well, McCrann and Aleck. He hadn't met wee mad Aleck, but his reputation was legendary,

The new Brief they had was also called McCrann just one of those things, I guess, well he was not afraid of ending up like his predecessor. He carried a small firearm that was loaded and ready to use. Everybody knew he had a gun and that left him with the responsibility that anyone who messed wae him were going to come of the worse. Gizmo carried on punting. He got rid of another ounce. That was sweet. He even sold a few tabs o' acid 'Jaggers'.

⚜

Grandad got his balaclava out and his straight cut razor. Cha got out his small Smith and Weston bulldog revolver. It was a six-shot barrel and weighed a little bit heavy. Raymie smiled at Cha as they were both dressed in black. It was two thirty in the morning and Pinkie honked his horn at the pair of them. Then they went straight in for Grandad, knowing full and well he was calling the shots. Grandad got down the stairs and into the back seat. The passengers side. Nobody said a word but to say they look menacing, well that was an understatement. Pinkie smiled as they parked just a little way off the guy's house and waited, it was four in the morning he left at about six. Grandad scowled at the guy's house.

Pinkie asked, "What if he's got kids?"

Grandad sighed, "He should of, thought of that before he made me and my rear his playground".

Cha smiled and they donned their balaclavas. Whilst the time was ticking away Beano and Skull were fulfilling their part in this diabolical plan. They were stood either side of the top pet's cell, one wae a blanket the other a chib. The cell door got opened and Beano and Skull rushed in wrapped the blanket around him and stabbed the fucking poofy cunt repeatedly. There were more than ten stab wounds as they rushed him.

Then as if it was ordained the screw Rafferty came out. They rushed rapidly at the guy crouching low and letting their arms flop naturally holding their weapons. Pinkie grabbed the fuck and Grandad sliced the boy repeatedly sending the blood everywhere. Then Cha shot him twice once on each kneecap. And Raymie kicked him in the nuts. But he was too busy trying to hold his face together. They then headed back to their wheels and drove off. Grandad looked at the razor that was covered in the viscose, liquid blood. They got dropped off and immediately threw their bloody rags into the big buckets at the bottom of their stairwell. James burned his out back and that was vengeance.

Grandad was up at Biscuits two days later and biscuit was happy tae see him after that. Knowing that they were kings in that jungle and that action just reinforced that fact. Kingo smiled as he saw Grandad and Pinkie coming his way on foot. It was the end to a cruel summer; the police finally got the message that the YBC were number one and that they were coming up roses everyway they could.

~ The End ~~